REMINISCE GHOST STORIES
BOOK 3

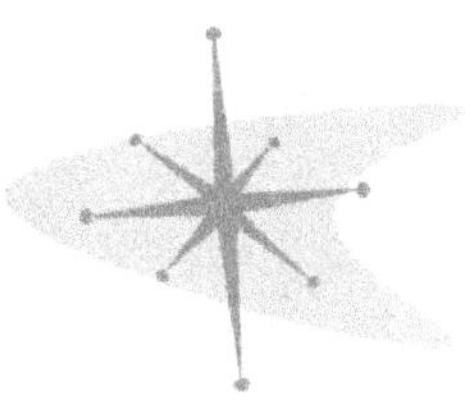

Reminisce line of books by Kirk House Publishers

For Mom

My beautiful mother, Mary

REMINISCE GHOST STORIES
BOOK 3

A Collection of Stories by Kirk House Publishers

First Edition
Paperback: 978-1-952976-96-4
eBook: 978-1-952976-97-1
Hardcover: 978-1-952976-98-8

Library of Congress Control Number: pending

Cover and Interior Design by Ann Aubitz
Images on cover from Book Brush

Published by Kirk House Publishers
1250 E 115th Street
Burnsville, MN 55337
Kirkhousepublishers.com
612-781-2815

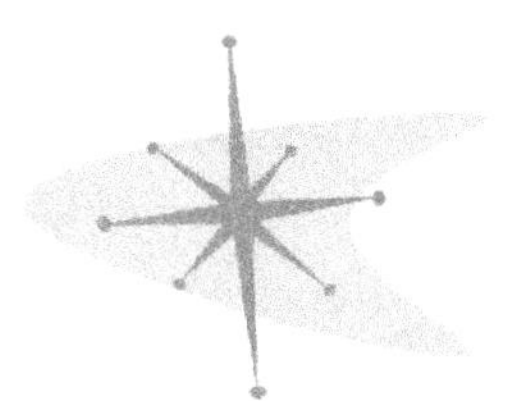

Foreword

When Ann Aubitz from Kirk House Publishers called me about the new line of books she was publishing for older readers, my ears perked up. I knew this was an underserved market. Ann explained her series would be different from the books currently available. Her books were actually inspired by an elder, her 96-year-old mother, who still enjoys reading.

I was excited to review the books myself, as so often, books for our elders have small print, they are hard to hold, or they have storylines that are too complicated to comprehend, or on the other side, they are overly simplified and childlike.

What I found was Ann's books (the Reminisce book line) were designed to be dignified and intriguing. In addition, they would meet multiple needs:

1. Large print for older eyes.
2. The larger-sized book makes it easier to hold, as it is common for fine motor skills to decline as we age.
3. Intriguing storylines for all ages. This allows flexibility to share intergenerationally, allowing grandma or grandpa to read to their grandchildren, or their grandkids can read the book to their grandparents, if they are in the mood to share.
4. Along the lines of intergenerational, the books also can teach children a bit about the past and to engage in conversation about the good old days that elders refer to.

5. These books are ideal for a wide range of people and abilities of various ages, and for those with early cognition issues, they are *ideal*!

The stories are set in the 1940s, 1950s, and 1960s in an easy-to-read, short-story format in the genres we love: mystery, romance, ghost stories, and science fiction. Large type and full-colored illustrations make the stories accessible to all readers, many of whom may have their own special memories of those periods of history.

This series will meet a wide range of needs, enabling many people who love to read to continue having that pleasure.

I highly recommend the Reminisce book line for your special someone that still loves to read.

~Lori La Bey, founder of Alzheimer's Speaks

Alzheimer's Speaks is a Minnesota-based advocacy group and media outlet making an international impact. Our goal is to shift dementia care from crisis to comfort by giving voice to all and raising those voices to enrich lives by sharing critical information, personal stories, resources, products, and tools from people and organizations at all levels around the world.

Website: https://alzheimersspeaks.com

Table of Contents

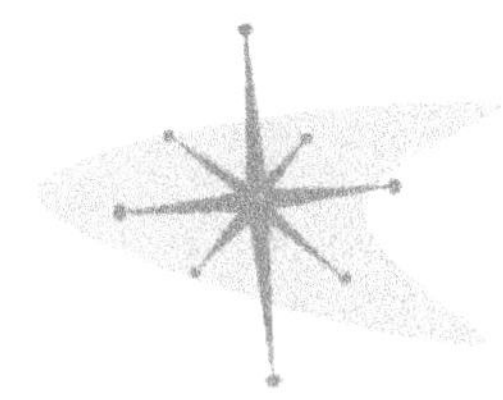

Introduction

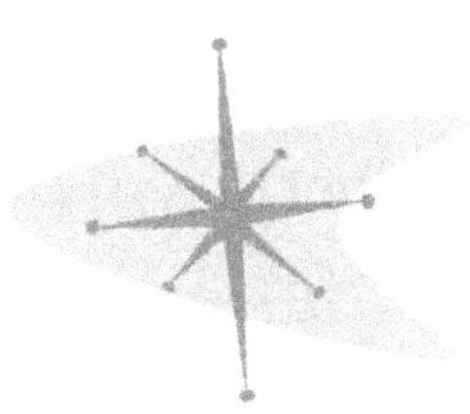

When I was young, the greatest joy for me was reading books. But, of course, this was before reading was cool like it is now. It was a time when my friends were playing their first computer games, but not me—my nose was always buried in a book. In those stories, I went to far-off places and had amazing adventures. In those stories, I could be free.

I credit my love of reading to my mom. Born in 1926 to a family with sixteen children, she never finished high school, but she had a thirst for knowledge and reading that thrived throughout the years.

I remember only a few times while growing up that my mom didn't have a book, magazine, or word puzzle in her hands—she had an insatiable quest for knowledge.

In her senior living facility library, she discovered a book that she loved. It was *Little Women*, by American novelist Louisa May Alcott. It was altered from the original book in a good way. This book contained illustrations and larger print. My mom would run her fingers over the pictures to remember a time long past. She read and reread the book.

Unfortunately for her, there were no other books like this in the library. She tried and failed to read books with more complex storylines and smaller type. She would get frustrated and distraught because reading no longer brought her joy.

This is why I started this line of books. It is for people like me and my mom that *love* to read. These books are meant to be easy to read, have a complete storyline, and help readers remember a time long past and *to reminisce.*

Kirk House Publishers is proud to present the Reminisce Line of reader-friendly books. Written by several authors, the stories are set in the 1940s, 1950s, and 1960s in an easy-to-read, short-story format. Large type and full-colored illustrations make the stories accessible to all readers, many of whom may have their own special memories of those periods of history.

Happy Reading!

~Ann Aubitz

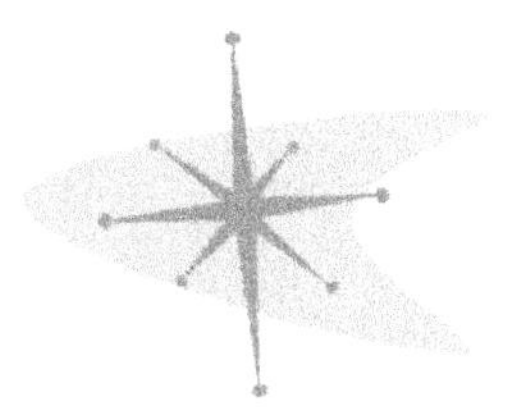

STORY ONE
The Harrington Hotel
His Broken Heart
By Ann Aubitz

He was running. He didn't know where he was running to, but he knew what he was running from. His life was falling apart—so he just ran.

Jim felt dizzy and thought he might black out. This whole situation started because of a fight with his fiancé. She told him that she had found someone new, so it wasn't exactly a fight but rather more of a statement that he wasn't good enough. Hell, he knew he wasn't good enough for her because her parents took every opportunity to remind him of that fact. He was the son of a criminal, and everyone in their highbrow east coast neighborhood knew it.

Jim thought about how he ended up here, lost, hungry, cold, and in the middle of nowhere...

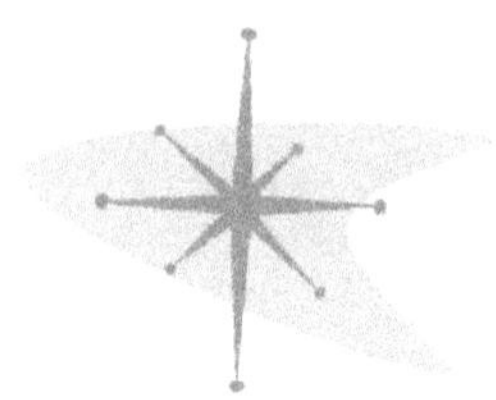

Jim and his fiancé Linda had pulled their car off on a remote dirt road. He thought they were going to make out and talk about their wedding that was planned for this summer. Linda was beautiful, rich, and funny, and he knew how lucky he was to be with her. The only downside to Linda were her parents, who clearly didn't think he was good enough for their little girl.

Earlier today, as he drove, he had noticed the change of seasons, the small piles of snow were melting, leaving way for new growth. It was early spring, and the little yellow flowers that populated the side of the road were in bloom and popping up all over. The leaves were budding on the trees, and the air had a fresh grassy smell. Spring had always been his favorite time of year, but now he would forever associate springtime with getting dumped by his girl just eight weeks before their wedding.

They drove for about an hour to get out of the city and pulled over by the side of the road. He turned his brand new

1953 dark blue Hudson Hornet off and put his arm around Linda. She pushed it aside as she turned to face him.

"What was that for?" Jim huffed.

"I don't want to kiss you. I want to talk to you."

"We could have talked the whole way here, but you didn't say two words to me." He was starting to lose his temper.

"I wanted to face you while I was telling you this."

"Well, what is it?" He asked impatiently.

Suddenly she appeared nervous and looked around at the remote location with trepidation. "Maybe we should drive back home, and then we can talk." She twisted her hands in her lap.

"You said you wanted to go for a ride in the country, so I took you for a ride, and now you want me to drive you back home?"

"Yes, I think that will be best." However, she stated it with more confidence than she felt.

"Best for who? Spit it out," he barked.

"I-I-I don't think we should get married." She had to push the words out of her mouth.

"What! Why? You were the one that insisted upon getting married." Now he knew he was losing his temper.

"I know. I still want to get married." She twisted a piece of her long blonde hair with her fingers, a trait he realized meant she was nervous.

"I get it. You just don't want to marry me." He said, feeling dismayed.

"I met someone else." She said so quietly that he could hardly hear her.

"Are you kidding me? You were the one that chased me! You were the one that wanted to get married after two months. I was happy just dating, and you insisted on a huge circus of a wedding with over four hundred guests." He felt as if he was losing his temper, so he took a deep breath and asked, "Do your parents know?"

"Yes, they know." Her green eyes were brimming with tears. He *almost* felt bad for her.

"And?" His tone was laced with sarcasm.

"Well, they aren't happy with me canceling this close to the wedding date. There are several deposits they aren't going to get back."

"That's what they are worried about, the money? Your dad is the richest person in the world."

"They think it's the right decision."

"Of course, they do. They have never approved of me." Now he *was* losing his temper. So, before he did something stupid, he got out of the car and walked down the dusty gravel road into the woods.

She rolled down the window, stuck her head out, and screamed, "Where are you going?"

"For a walk, you can take the car. I'm sure your dad will want it back."

She said something else, but he was too far away to hear. He started running until his lungs burned, and he was forced to stop. He looked around but didn't recognize his surroundings. The sparse woods where they parked was now thick, dense foliage. The gravel path disappeared about a half mile ago, so he was making his own path. Running and stumbling over tree roots as he ran full steam.

He stopped and leaned back on a tree. The sky had gotten dark and the forest thick, and he had no idea where he was. That's when he realized he was in trouble.

Jim awoke to the sound of his own teeth chattering. The last thing he remembered was leaning against the tree trunk to catch his breath. Now he found himself under the tree, frozen to the ground where he lay.

"Get up." He heard a whisper in the wind. "Get up now."

"Dad?"

He thought he heard his dad's voice telling him to get up. But that was impossible. His dad was in prison for embezzling money from the medical manufacturing company he worked for. His dad was an executive at the company and discovered that the owners he worked for used substandard parts, and people were dying. But instead of going to the police, he figured out a way to steal the money and give it to the families who had lost a loved one. Unfortunately, although it was admirable, he still went to prison for the theft.

"Hurry." The voice said again.

He struggled to get to a sitting position, then used the base of the trunk to pull himself up. He stumbled for a moment and then was on his feet. The sky was black as tar, but the moon shone brightly and lit the way.

Jim got his footing and wrapped his arms around his midsection to warm himself. He stumbled about 100 feet and swore he saw a large house in the distance. It was the last thought before blackness enveloped him, and he slumped to the ground.

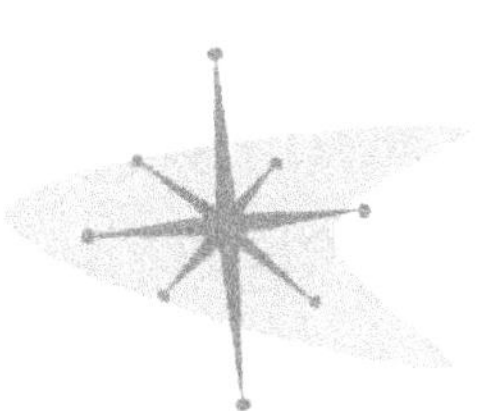

"Is he dead?" Jim vaguely registered the voice of a young woman. His first thought was that it was Linda, but his heart knew the truth. Linda had moved on, and he thought he wanted to die.

"No, Maryann, he's still alive, but just barely. I'm sure he has hypothermia. I bet he has been out here all night."

"But why?"

"I don't know, honey, but I do know that the house wants us to save him. So, let's get him inside."

Jim, tried to speak, but nothing came out, and he couldn't open his eyes. He didn't understand the last thing the man said but was relieved someone had found him.

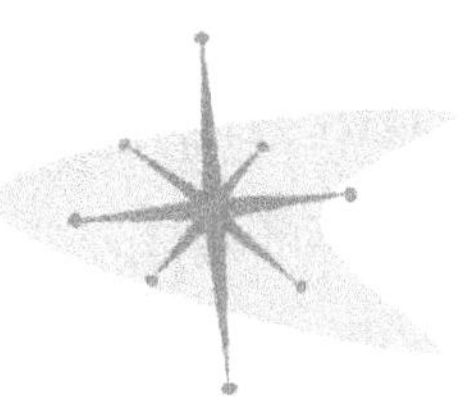

Maryann had cared for the handsome stranger for a week, and he hadn't opened his eyes once. Several times she thought he was dead and had put a mirror in front of his mouth to ensure he was still breathing. Each time his breath fogged up the mirror, she felt relieved. His breath was shallow but steady, and it seemed a little better every day—but he didn't seem to have the will to live.

She wasn't sure what to do. She didn't want him to die. She envisioned him in her life—even though she didn't know him. But, in her twenty-one years, she had never encountered someone this close to death. So, she did what she thought was best. She talked to him. She read that people in a coma and close to death could hear people's voices, so she just talked about everything she could think of.

"Good morning, Jim Cooper. I hope you had a good night." This is how she started all her conversations with him. They knew his name because of his driver's license. Her father had gotten the stranger out of his cold, wet clothes and put him in a pair of PJs to be more comfortable. Although it was spring, the temperature at night dipped below freezing, and his toes and fingers were frostbitten. She hoped he wouldn't lose the use of his fingers and toes, but she would never know if he didn't wake up.

"Today, I promised to tell you the story about our mansion. We call it a hotel now, but it is not a normal hotel." She thought she saw a flicker of movement in his eyelashes. "My father bought this place from an old man and his wife for one dollar. I know it sounds crazy, but that is all it cost him. The stipulation was that he could never leave. I know that part does sound crazy. It didn't mean he couldn't run to the store to get something. It meant he couldn't leave the house in someone else's care for an extended period or outright leave it uninhabited."

This time she did see Jim's face move a bit, he hadn't moved in the week since they found him, and she was getting worried. There was no medical reason for his paralysis. If she blamed something, she would blame heartache. On the first day, he called out the name Linda several times, but since then, nothing. It was like he resigned himself to the fact that he had lost her.

Maryann knew that the hotel would help Jim. She often saw how their place helped people. They had guests who needed to reconnect with loved ones, both alive and dead. She glanced at Jim's face and knew the situation with him seemed a little different, but she still hoped the house could help him.

She realized she had stopped talking and that he seemed agitated by this fact. "Okay, so back to my story. My dad played in these woods as a boy, never seeing this mansion. We know now that the house only reveals itself to people who need help. When my father was older, he walked along the trail and finally saw the house. You see, he was at a crossroads in his life, much like you are now. The woman he thought he would marry fell in love with another. So, my dad was walking in the woods to clear his head and came upon my grandfather and his daughter chopping wood in the clearing."

She stopped for a dramatic pause.

"See, at that time, my grandfather knew that people couldn't see the house unless they needed to—unless the house could help them. So, when my father, Mervin, mentioned seeing the house, my grandfather knew it was meant to be. My grandfather also noticed the looks between his daughter, Gloria, and the stranger, and figured it was the house making things happen."

Maryann paused the story again to look at herself in the mirror directly across the room. Her dad always said she was the spitting image of her mom at her age, with curly brown hair that never behaved, bright blue eyes, and a cute button nose smattered with freckles. She stopped looking at herself in the mirror and looked into Jim's handsome face. She didn't think that Jim would find her attractive, but again she would never know if he didn't wake up. Suddenly he seemed more animated and alive than he had been since he got there. He seemed as if he was listening intently to her story. Feeling hopeful that he would wake up, she continued with her tale.

"So, Grandpa George sold my dad the mansion for one dollar. Once they signed the papers, the hotel was his. My father knew that the person taking over the hotel had to agree to stay until the next person was chosen by the house to take over. You may be asking where my mom came into this story. Well, my mom was George's daughter, Gloria, and she fell in love with dad from the first moment she saw him."

A single tear ran down Maryann's face as she remembered her mother.

"My mom didn't understand that she had to stay forever. She didn't believe in the power of the house. She thought her dad made up the story to scare her and her new husband into staying. She ignored the signs and the stories from her father and made her plan to leave. So, one night shortly after I was born, she packed up all her belongings and tried to leave the house with me. Dad wouldn't go with her and begged her to stay. He wasn't sure what the house would do to them if they broke the contract, they both signed."

Maryann stopped and stared out the window, stuck in her own thoughts about the past.

"What happened to your mom?" He croaked. When Jim spoke these words, Maryann jumped a foot in the air. His voice came out more of a rasp than a full voice. When Maryann didn't answer, he repeated his question.

"What happened to her?" He spoke a little louder this time.

Maryann looked at him with disbelief because he hadn't spoken a word since that first day he called out Linda's name. Finally, she decided to finish the story, get her father, and tell him their patient was awake.

"She was walking down the stairs and fell."

"Is that how she died?"

"No, she didn't die that night but was hurt badly. She had to use a wheelchair for the rest of her life. She passed away last year when she got pneumonia. My dad says that she was never the same after the fall." Maryann started to weep, then Jim took her hand in his softly.

"She insisted that someone pushed her down the stairs. She said that an older man and woman appeared like magic at the top of the stairs, and they told her she couldn't leave, then pushed her down the flight of stairs. My father stood there holding me in his arms but didn't see anyone."

"Wow, that is quite a story." Jim looked at Maryann in disbelief.

"Yes, it is."

A month later...

Jim was up and about helping Mervin and Maryann run the Inn. It was the most useful and happiest he had ever felt in his whole life.

"Take it easy big boy. You just got back on your feet." Jim loved the way Maryann flirted with him. They had a lot of fun together; she had a fantastic sense of humor and was cute as a button.

"I will, bossy pants. I want to bring some wood into the house for our next guests in case they want a fire in the fireplace in their rooms."

"Okay, but they won't be here until sometime tomorrow, so don't overdo it, or you'll end up back in bed."

"I'm just going to run this bundle upstairs to room 201. Then I will be done for the day—I promise."

"Okay, but don't make me come up and get you," Maryann said as she walked over to the registry at the front desk. That was strange. Jim Cooper's name was at the top of the list for check-ins today, but he had been there for weeks and was assigned to room 201, the same room he was heading to.

"Dad, come quick!"

"What is it, honey?"

"Look at this."

"What?"

"This, right here, is Jim's name. he is scheduled as a guest for today in room 201, and that is where he just brought the bundle of wood."

"Honey, I have learned after all these years that the house knows what is best for people."

They didn't speak for a few minutes, then Maryann said, "What do you think is happening with Jim? I don't want anything bad to happen to him."

"Honey, he has unfinished business with his ex-fiancé. He can't move forward with you until he sorts it out. I know you think highly of him."

"Dad, I'm in love with him."

Her dad looked at her with surprise. He had never heard those words come out of his daughter's mouth.

"Don't look so shocked. You knew it had to happen sometime."

"Yes, but I don't think a father is ever ready to hear those words. But I must say if it had to be someone, I am glad it is Jim. He is a good man."

Jim headed down the hallway to room 201. He thought about his last few weeks and his new lease on life. He discovered that he loved the Inn and working with his hands. Chopping wood was his new favorite chore because it gave him time to think. During his wood chopping sessions, he realized that he was never really in love with Linda and that he had dodged a bullet. He was starting to feel that Maryann was the one for him.

He got to the door and, out of habit, knocked before going in. He opened the door and nearly dropped the bundle. A gorgeous blond was sitting in the high-backed Victorian chair in the middle of the room.

"About time you're back. Where did you go to get the wood? On the moon?"

"Linda, what the hell are you doing here?"

"What do you mean what am I doing here?"

"Well, when I left you a few weeks ago, you told me you were in love with someone else and broke our engagement."

"I wish!" she said dubiously, "I don't know what you are talking about. Did you hit your head when you got the wood? We've been married for two years now. We're celebrating our second anniversary, and you bring me to this godforsaken place."

"Our what?"

"Why are you acting so weird? Well, weirder than normal." Then she added in a hushed tone, "My parents were right about you."

"What did you say?"

"I said that my parents were right about you. We've spent the last two years fighting."

"About what?"

"About my money."

"We have?"

"What is wrong with you? We got married two years ago. Ever since that day, you have wandered from one job to the next, never settling in. My father even hired you at his firm for a great wage and a corner office, and you made a scene the very first day and lost your job. It's like you aren't even trying to support us. Then you drag me to this horrible place for our second anniversary, and you wonder why I am not happy. Should I go on?"

"No, that's enough. I am sorry, Linda. I shouldn't have agreed to marry you, and I should have stopped this much sooner. We were never a good fit. I was so taken with your beauty and, to be honest, your money, that I thought we could work it out, but money doesn't solve everything."

"No, it doesn't." Her eyes softened when she looked at him.

"Thank you, Jim, for saying that. It means a lot to me. I guess I will be going now."

"Good luck to you, Linda. I hope you find what you're looking for."

They hugged, then Linda turned away from him and disappeared. He could still smell her expensive perfume lingering in the room.

He stood there for a moment remembering the story Maryann told him about the house, knowing what you needed. He needed to forgive himself and Linda for their mistakes so he could move on with Maryann. He couldn't deny that he had fallen in love with her throughout the last few weeks. Maybe that was the house's doing too, but she was so impressive that he figured he would love her no matter where they were.

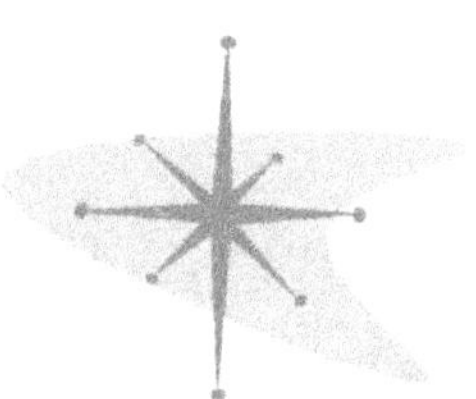

Maryann busied herself downstairs, straightening up the common rooms and preparing the main rooms for their new guests. She didn't expect Jim to come down for some time. Maybe the house was reuniting him with Linda. Maybe that was what was supposed to happen. Maryann didn't always understand the house's magic, and she liked it better that way.

She knew that staying at the house was her destiny and that the house took care of people—gave them what they needed whether they wanted it or not.

Suddenly she heard a noise behind her and realized that Jim was coming down the stairs. When she turned around to face him, she stopped in her tracks. They just stared at each other for a moment, and they both knew that they were destined to be together forever, and this place would be their forever home— The Harrington Hotel.

STORY TWO
The Harrington Hotel
Lost Love
By Ann Aubitz

He wasn't exactly sure where he was driving but instinctively knew it was the right way. So, he drove in the blackness of the night, down the narrow dirt road, and through the thick dark forest. After what seemed like a hundred miles, the road finally opened up to a clearing filled with a dense fog. He carefully pulled to the side of the road to calculate his next step.

He strained to see, but it was useless; nothing was visible in this pea soup. Suddenly the fog lifted, and he was in front of one of the largest, most frightening mansions he had ever seen. The house was surrounded by a ten-foot-tall wrought iron fence, the sharp peaks at the top made to ward off unwanted guests. Reluctantly he got out of the car to open the gate, but before he could reach it, the gate opened on its own.

He drove his car around the perfectly manicured grounds and parked in front of the house. A few minutes passed before he got out of his car, went up the walkway, and stood at the front door. He lifted his hand to the door knocker, but the door opened before he could announce himself. The dark wood double doors revealed a large foyer with an enormous desk, and a pleasant-looking young woman who stood behind it.

"Good evening, sir. You must be Mr. Nicholas Hager. My name is Maryann Metz, soon to be Maryann Cooper." She held up her left hand and wiggled her fingers to show him her ring, but at this moment, he couldn't care less about anyone's happiness. He was miserable, bewildered, and unsure of where or why he was there. He ignored her comment about her impending marriage and asked, "What is this place?"

"You are a guest at The Harrington Hotel, Mr. Hager."

Nicholas looked around at the extravagant furnishings and wondered how and why he was at this strange place. Maybe his new boss was treating him to a vacation because he saw how hard he was working. Oh, but this was a peculiar place. He could hear a buzzing in his ears and feel a pulse moving through his body. This house certainly had a strange effect on his nervous system.

"I still don't understand. One minute I was at home eating a TV dinner, and the next moment I found myself driving up to this place."

"The best way for me to explain this is to say that the house knows what you need. Only people that need something in their life are brought to us."

He just stared at her as if he didn't understand her words. Then, finally, she jiggled the keys in front of his face to get his attention.

"Here are your keys, sir. You are in room 202, which is up the stairs and to the right. I will have Jim bring your luggage up so you can go ahead and relax."

"Fine." He was irritated and hated feeling out of control. There was only one other time in his life when he felt this out of control: when he was a young man in Paris, he had a similar feeling, which didn't end well.

He trudged up the massive marble staircase and turned to the right when he got to the top of the stairs. He faced a wide hallway with dark ornate wood carvings that stretched from floor to ceiling. When he moved closer to them, he grew dizzy and put his hand on the wall to steady himself. He could feel the wall pulsating like a rapid heartbeat beneath his fingers. He quickly moved his hand away and continued down the hallway toward his room.

"I bet I am having an anxiety attack. Maybe I should leave?" He said out loud, but no one else was there, so he was surprised when someone answered.

"You're fine, and everything will be okay." A haunting male voice crooned.

"Oh, great, now I'm hearing voices. Now I know I'm having an anxiety attack or maybe even a heart attack. That's what I get for working so hard for the last thirty years. Never taking time for myself, my nose always to the grindstone. So this is what I get for my troubles, a nervous breakdown."

He stumbled to room 202. He was having a difficult time getting the key in the keyhole.

"Relax," The haunting voice said again. It seemed to be coming from the opposite end of the hallway.

"Hello, who's there? I demand that you show yourself," he said with a false sense of confidence. His breathing was rapid, and his hands were shaking.

Nicholas heard no response, so he turned the key and opened the door as quickly as possible. Instead of seeing the general fare for hotel rooms: beds, chairs, and dressers, his hotel room door opened to Paris, France, more specifically, the café he frequented when he was a young man living in the city. The scene before him brought bittersweet memories. Paris was where he met his one true love almost thirty years ago. He was supposed to meet her in this very café but left the country without saying goodbye. His once-in-a-lifetime love was Chloé, and she was extraordinary.

The year was 1923, and he was his best twenty-five-year-old self – he had a relatively high opinion of himself, as all his friends would say. What they didn't know was that he came from a horrible upbringing. His father was drunk and abusive and beat both him and his mother. Once Nicholas reached the age where he was as robust as his father, he started challenging him. His father knew he couldn't win a fight against Nicholas, so his dad left, never to return.

He and his mother were fine on their own for the most part. She refused to go to her family for help, so they relied on each other and the kindness of their friends. He could have had it worse—at least he had one parent who loved him. Unfortunately, she died when he was fourteen, and he ended up at an orphanage until he ran away from that life at seventeen years old, never to look back.

He swore to his mother on her death bed that he would make something of himself. No one would ever treat him like crap again. He started working at a manufacturing company in the mail room when he was eighteen, worked his way up to lead salesperson, and then got offered a job in Paris. He moved to France, not listening to anything his colleagues told him about the country. They mentioned that he should learn the language and the culture because it would go a long way in helping him acclimate to the country. He brushed off their suggestions, thinking he knew best. He had better things to do than sit in a library learning to speak French.

Although, in hindsight, he wished he would have listened to them. Maybe if he had, he wouldn't have been lost all the time, but then, he wouldn't have met her—Chloé.

After his little walk down memory lane, he realized he was still standing with the door partially open into the hallway. He felt like he was being pulled toward the café, toward Chloé, but this couldn't be right. This must be part of his mental breakdown, and he was becoming delusional. The weird thing was, in addition to being able to see Paris, the smells and the sounds of Paris were also rushing to his senses. The smell of the croissants, the coffee, and the loud hum of the traffic was all around him.

Nicholas stumbled forward as if someone pushed him, and the door closed with a thud. As he turned toward the door, it disappeared.

He decided that as long as his mind was playing tricks on him, he would like to play along and visit the café. It had been too long since he had good French pastries and coffee. So he walked down the cobblestone street and passed by a women's dress shop. The styles sure were outdated for 1953. Everything looked as he remembered from 1923, even his reflection in the store window.

"Oh no, now I know I have gone crazy. Nicholas stared at his reflection in the mirror and saw his 25-year-old self, staring back at him. He ran his hand down his face and tried to wipe the image away to no avail.

"Bonne après-midi Nicolas." The server said from the patio outside the café. "Qu'est ce que je peux vous servir?"

"What can you get for me?" Nicolas was more confused than ever. This woman who spoke to him was the waitress he and Chloé knew from the café all those years ago. But it couldn't be. She looked the same as she did the last time he saw her, nearly thirty years ago.

"Oui, Nicholas. Chloé has your table saved, go ahead and sit down and I will be right back."

The waitress motioned to the table at the edge of the patio overlooking the Seine River. It was his and Chloé's favorite spot in the whole city. They came here the first day they met and just about every day thereafter.

He was looking around the patio, hoping to see Chloé, but knowing that this was only his imagination and not real. But, even if it wasn't real, it would sure be nice to see her again. To hold her, to nuzzle his face in her neck and smell her expensive Parisian perfume.

"Bonjour Nicholas." It was *his* Chloé as she was in 1923, tall, brunette, gorgeous, full of life, and unique. In all the years since he left her, he had never found another woman like her. He stood as she approached the table. She came to him and kissed him on both cheeks, as was the custom in Paris. He moved his mouth to her lips and wrapped his arms around her in a loving embrace.

"Wow, you are happy to see me." She said with her heavily accented English.

"It has been so long, and I've missed you so much."

"It was only yesterday, at this very table, in fact."

"Well, it—um—um, feels longer when I am not with you." He stuttered through his sentence, not really sure what he should share with her about his situation. She would think he was crazy. "I am sorry. Please sit down." He held out the chair for her.

"Merci, Nicholas." The way she said his name was lyrical. He had forgotten how much he loved listening to her speak.

"It is just so good to see you. How have you been?"

"You are worrying me, Nicholas. Not much has happened since I saw you last night. Are you okay?"

"I am now. I needed this in my life to see you again and remember how happy I was here."

"I am so glad, and I hope all our plans for the future come true."

"Oh, what plans are those?"

"Of you staying in Paris, of course, and running my family's hotel with me. It would be a glorious life, just you and me at the Inn. No more long hours at your company or being gone for days at a time in meetings, just you and me together forever."

"Hmmm, I had forgotten that's what we talked about."

"What do you mean forgotten? We have been talking about it every day for more than a year. You seemed excited about our plan and living in Paris with me."

"You know I was offered a sales promotion in our company's German division. Don't you want to come with me to Germany?"

"What is going on, Nicholas?" She raised her voice, and several other patrons began to take notice. "Why are you saying this now? We had plans, you and I."

"I think we should look at all our avenues before deciding on the rest of our lives. We could miss something bigger and better."

"What's bigger and better than our love?" She shrieked, now everyone at the café was staring at them.

"Chloé, don't be like that."

"Like what? Don't be in love with you? We have been talking about this for a year. You have never mentioned that you were looking for something bigger and better in your life than me. So maybe we should take a break until you figure out what you really want. Your career or me."

"But why do I have to choose? Why can't I have both?"

"Because I don't want to live that way. Me waiting all night for you to come home. Me reheating your food over and over because you are late. Me being alone for days at a time because you are out of town. I just don't want to live like that."

"But you are asking me to give up the biggest opportunity of my life."

"I thought you said I was the biggest opportunity of your life? Nicholas, you need to do what you think is right. Let's meet back here in a week. If you want to leave, go with my blessing, but I will not be with you. I don't want the life you seem to crave."

"But Chloé."

"No, Nicholas. I will see you next week."

She walked away. As she did, he remembered this was exactly the way it happened last time. If he was given a second chance, he just blew it.

Last time, he left Paris before the week was up. He never met her, never tried to contact her until it was too late. A couple of years later, he was in Paris and heard from a mutual friend that she had married and had children. He had never forgotten her; no woman ever measured up to her. His position in Germany was terrible, and he ended up leaving the company. Since then, he had been wandering from job to job, trying to make ends meet, never having found the peace he had in Paris. Finally, he realized that the single biggest mistake in his life was leaving Chloé the first time, and he just did it again.

He looked around at his surroundings and found that he was sitting on a chair in the middle of the hotel room. The bed was against the far wall. His luggage was next to the door. He held his head in his hands and realized that his Paris dream had slipped away from him again.

Nicholas stood, walked across the room, grabbed his luggage, and opened the door, knowing that Chloé was his chance at happiness, and he made the same mistake twice. Would he ever learn? He would give anything for one more chance with Chloé.

He pulled his heavy luggage down the flight of stairs and stepped into the foyer, looking for the young woman he had met earlier this evening. But instead, he came upon a middle-aged woman standing in the foyer staring straight at him. She was tall, brunette, gorgeous, full of life, and unique, a little bit older, but...

"No, it can't be. Chloé?"

"Bonjour Nicholas!"

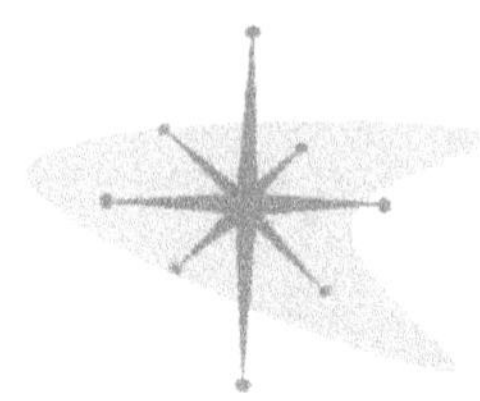

Two months later...

Nicholas and Chloé were married outside the café where they first met. Chloé was widowed a few years earlier after an amazing life, and now Nicholas had a chance for an amazing life too. He wasn't going to mess up his Paris Dream again.

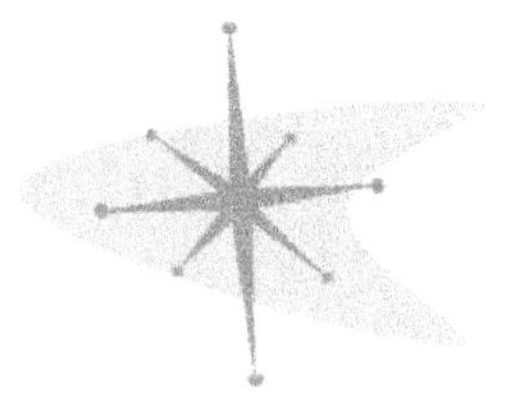

STORY THREE
The Harrington Hotel
Friends Forever
By Ann Aubitz

They planned a trip to Mexico for their thirtieth birthdays but ended up here instead…

"Why are we here again?" Jennifer bellowed.

"You heard the guy at the airport. The fog has all the flights grounded, so he said he would put us in a hotel for the night." Paul explained the situation for what seemed like the umpteenth time. Both women hounded him the whole way here. No, actually, it was just one of the women, Jennifer. The other woman he traveled with was still as sweet as when they were kids. On the way here, he wasn't sure where he was driving. But he instinctively knew it was the right way.

"I heard what he said, but do you really think this is the hotel he had in mind? Jennifer said with a bite to her words.

"I agree with Jennifer. This just doesn't seem right. It felt like we drove for a hundred miles." Elizabeth stated quietly.

"It did seem that way, but based on his directions, I drove the way I thought we should go. If you didn't like it, one of you could have driven through this godforsaken fog. I would have gladly let you."

The three friends were standing in the house's foyer but didn't see the woman behind the desk. Suddenly she was there as if she had appeared out of nowhere.

"Oh heavens," Elizabeth sighed, seeing Maryann for the first time.

"Hello and welcome to The Harrington Hotel, I am your host Maryann Conner, and you must be Miss Smith, Miss Miller, and Mr. Davis. We have been expecting you."

"See, I told you we were in the right place." Paul was smug. He was rarely told he was right with Jennifer around, so he figured he would enjoy it.

"You most definitely are, Mr. Davis."

"Please call me Paul. What is this place, Miss Conner?"

"It is Mrs., but please call me Maryann. The Harrington Hotel has been in my family for three generations; before that, the mansion was owned by a very wealthy family. My grandfather turned it into a hotel so the beauty of the place could be shared with everyone."

"It certainly is beautiful," exclaimed Elizabeth, turning around in a circle to take in the splendor of the entire room.

"Thank you. We are very proud of it." Maryann rechecked the registry. It seems as if you are booked for three nights."

"No, that isn't right. We are supposed to fly out tomorrow to Mexico." Jennifer snapped at Maryann.

"Oh, sorry, my mistake." She rechecked the registry and grabbed three sets of keys from the wall behind her. She handed a key to each one of them.

Jennifer handed her key back to Maryann. "Maryann, Elizabeth, and I will share a room."

"The house—oops, I—I mean, we have plenty of room so you can each enjoy one of your own. Your rooms are on the second floor. Please go up the staircase; on the left, you will see your three rooms in a row. My husband Jim will bring your luggage upstairs. So please go on ahead and relax."

They walked away from the desk toward the staircase.

"Well, she was odd." Jennifer barked.

"Shhh, Jennifer, she could hear you." Paul reprimanded her.

They turned to see if Maryann was still there, but she was gone as quickly as she came into the room.

"Doesn't this whole situation seem really weird? We are on our way to Mexico, the fog suddenly rolls in, and now we end up at a very creepy-looking mansion. I really don't think this is the hotel the airport would send us to. For one thing, it has to be ridiculously expensive."

"I agree with Jennifer."

"You always agree with Jennifer," Paul said under his breath.

"What is that supposed to mean?" Elizabeth whined.

"It means that every time Jennifer says something, you say, I agree with Jennifer," Paul retorted.

"Well, I usually do agree with Jennifer," Elizabeth muttered.

"Would you two please stop fighting? This is why we haven't gotten together since our high school days." Jennifer shouted to get their attention.

"I don't think this is the only reason we haven't gotten together," he said under his breath. "Fine, let's get upstairs and get to bed. We have a long drive back to the airport tomorrow, and we don't want to miss our flight." Paul started moving toward the staircase.

"That's for sure. I don't want to stay here longer than necessary—this place gives me the creeps." Jennifer said as she moved in line after Paul.

"It will be fine for one night. Come on, let's get a move on."

"Okay, we are coming," Elizabeth said.

They walked up the marble staircase and turned to the left as Maryann directed them. The moment they stepped onto the second floor, they all felt different. It was as if an electric current was moving through their bodies.

"I feel weird." Jennifer rubbed her hands up and down her arms to take the electrical feeling away.

"Me too," Elizabeth said.

"I am surprised you didn't say I agree with Jennifer."

"Paul, knock it off. You're being an ass." Jennifer gave him a mean look and kept rubbing her arms.

"Fine, I am going to my room. I will see the two of you in the morning." Paul stomped off.

"Good night, Paul." Elizabeth waved as Paul turned away. She hoped they could stay up and talk for a while like they did in the olden days.

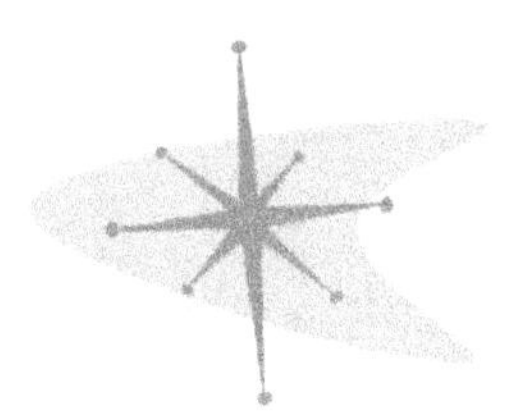

Paul knew he was being an ass, but he now remembered why he didn't hang around them anymore. They had all been the best of friends since they were toddlers. They lived on the same street and went to all the same schools. So, while other boys his age were out playing kickball and football, he hung out with Lizzie and Jenny. They would play for hours on end. But, most of the time, it was a game of dress-up or putting on a talent show for the neighborhood. He credited them with his impressive acting career. For the last ten years, he had been living in Hollywood, starred in several hit movies, and dated the most famous starlets. He was even rumored to be dating Jane Russell, although that was a lie. There was only one woman he loved, and she was standing out in the hallway of this hotel.

"Good riddance to him. He was a crab. Maybe he has outgrown us now that he is a big movie star, "Jennifer snapped.

"I don't think he acts differently. He is still the same old Paul." Elizabeth looked down at her feet when she spoke, hoping not to upset Jennifer any further. She was always watching what she said around Jennifer. They were best friends when they were young, but Jennifer started treating her like a lesser being when they hit puberty.

"You don't know what you are talking about. Didn't you hear the way he spoke to us?" Jennifer roared louder as the conversation continued.

"It wasn't to us, it was to you, and you have been riding him since this trip started. So, ease up a little bit." Finally, Elizabeth felt she could speak her mind.

"What? Who are you to tell me what to do?" Now Jennifer was incensed.

"I thought I was your best friend. And as your best friend, I am telling you that you need to relax. So go to your room, and I will see you in the morning." Elizabeth never felt stronger or more in control of a situation in her life. She had never felt this way with anyone, least of all Jennifer.

Jennifer was about to say something else to Elizabeth, but it was as if she suddenly couldn't form the words. It was a horrible feeling. She turned away from Elizabeth and headed toward her room.

Paul

As soon as Paul entered his hotel room, he heard kids' voices and was overwhelmed by the scent of school. The smell brought back memories of cafeteria lunches, sweaty locker rooms, and musty textbooks. He looked around to get his bearings and determined he was back in the gym at Lincoln High School, and the year was 1941. If he was correct, this was the night of the dance and the moment that everything changed between him, Jennifer, and Elizabeth. How the hell did I get here, he thought.

He walked down the hallway toward the gymnasium, where the last dance was happening. Tomorrow there would be a big carnival on the school grounds, and he had been looking forward to it for months. Finally, it was the day he had been waiting for when he could tell Elizabeth he was in love with her. He had waited until the end of the school year because he didn't want to upset their friendship—it meant too much. But now he knew it was the right time. Jennifer was going to nursing school out east, and Elizabeth was going to stay in their hometown and work at her father's restaurant. And well, he was going off to try his hand at this acting thing in Hollywood. Everyone said he had the face for it and was very theatrical.

He peered into the gymnasium and thought he must be having a mental breakdown. He saw his younger self dancing with Jennifer. Then, he remembered that this was the point in the evening where everything started unraveling. He was so excited that night that he blurted out his intentions to Jennifer: he would declare his love to Elizabeth. He told Jennifer that he would ask Elizabeth to go to Hollywood with him to start their new life.

He watched his younger self tell Jennifer his plans while they were on the dance floor. He didn't catch her facial expressions when he was an inexperienced eighteen-year-old, but he sure did now. Jennifer was congratulating him, but her face told him a different story. He was just too dumb then to pay attention to such things. She looked pea green with envy. How is it that he never noticed it before now? He watched as she left the dance floor under the guise of going to get a glass of punch. Instead, he watched her walk past him in the hallway and run into the girl's bathroom.

Paul listened outside the door as Jennifer told Elizabeth lie after lie. He listened intently, but then he was so mad that he burst into the girl's bathroom. He saw young Jennifer and young Elizabeth. Then everything went dark.

Jennifer

As soon as Jennifer entered her hotel room, she heard kids snickering and was overwhelmed by the scent of the sweaty socks in the gymnasium. Whoever thought they could add a few crepe paper streamers and twinkly lights and think this place looked better didn't know what they were doing. Decorations wouldn't fix this dump. She was so glad to be rid of this place and this good-for-nothing town.

She looked around with disgust when she realized she was back in the gym at Lincoln High School, and the year was 1941. How did I get back here, she wondered. She remembered this night. It was the night of the dance and the night that she changed everything between the three friends. She remembered being so excited to leave this town and move to New York City. She was going to nursing school and was going to ask Paul to come with her to try auditioning for parts on Broadway. She planned to have him live with her and see how things progressed. Because it was common knowledge that he didn't date, and she knew that between her and Elizabeth, she was far prettier and had way more to offer a man like Paul. Elizabeth was plain looking, mousy, unsure of herself, and always deferred to Jennifer. So, since Paul didn't date, she surmised that he was saving himself for her.

She watched her younger self dance with Paul. She remembered trying to get closer to him and how he kept backing away to keep some room between them. She wanted him to know her intentions and what she had planned, but he started talking first. She was proud of herself for controlling her facial expressions and disguising her disgust at his plan. Well, she would fix him.

Jennifer watched as her younger self marched into the girl's bathroom to tell Elizabeth that Paul despised her. Well, that will fix them, she thought. Jennifer had a smile on her face as she watched young Elizabeth sob.

Elizabeth

As soon as Elizabeth entered her hotel room, she heard kids laughing and was inundated with the fantastic scents of school. The unique smell brought back great memories of the noisy lunchroom, school supplies, and exciting classes. She looked around and knew she was back in the gym at Lincoln High School, and the year was 1941. This was the best time of her life, and she was so excited to be back. But how could it be? If she was right, this was the night of the dance and the night that her dreams were destroyed.

She walked down the long hallway and dreaded what she would see on the dance floor. She knew from what Jennifer told her that night that Paul confessed that he never cared for her and was glad to be rid of her. Elizabeth watched the scene unfold as Jennifer asked Paul to dance. That's strange.

Jennifer told her that Paul begged her to dance, and that Jennifer declined, saying she was waiting for Elizabeth.

As she watched, things became clear in her mind. She heard everything that Paul said, and not a word of it sounded anything like what Jennifer told her that night nearly twelve years ago.

Paul, Elizabeth, and Jennifer simultaneously walked out of their hotel rooms' doors. The air was thick with unresolved feelings.

Surprisingly it was Elizabeth who spoke first. "How could you do that to me? You had to have known how I felt about Paul."

Before Jennifer could speak, Paul said, "How did you feel about me, Lizzie?"

"Wait, don't answer," interrupted Jennifer. "Don't you remember all those terrible things he said about you the night of the dance Lizzie?"

"Don't call me Lizzie. That is reserved for my friends. I can't believe you did that to me, you made me feel horrible, and not just that night, but for the last twelve years, you have made me feel less of a person because of what you did that night."

"Oh boo-hoo! Go tell it to your shrink."

"Jennifer, that's enough." Then, Paul yelled, "Say you are sorry for what you have put Lizzie through."

"I am not going to apologize for your mistake. You should have picked me. I was and am better than she will ever be."

"No, Jennifer, you are not! You are mean and cruel, and I want nothing to do with you." Elizabeth got up in Jennifer's face and stood her ground.

"Who do you think you are?"

"Well, I know who I am not. I am not your best friend."

"Well, I never. You two are lucky to have me as a friend...." As Jennifer continued her tirade, Paul and Elizabeth watched as Jennifer started disappearing from her feet to the top of her head.

"Well good riddance." Elizabeth said, smiling.

"Aren't you the least bit upset about what we just saw?"

"Nope, I am just glad she is gone."

"Me too. Now I can do what I have wanted for twelve years." He bent down and gave Lizzie a loving kiss.

"What do you say we hang around here for a couple of days? This place is amazing!" Elizabeth wrapped her hands around Paul's neck and gave him another big kiss.

They walked hand in hand down the stairs and to the front desk to tell Maryann they would stay for three days.

"I knew you both would stay," said Maryann. "The house is never wrong."

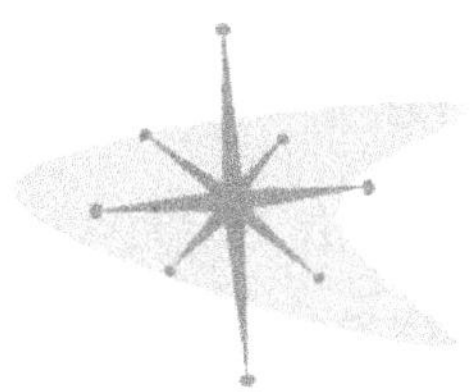

STORY FOUR
The Harrington Hotel
Hiding Out
By Ann Aubitz

Knock, knock, knock. The sound echoed through the hallway. "Mr. Jones, are you in there?"

He knew why she was outside his door. She wanted him to leave the hotel and join the human race again. But he didn't want to leave here yet, and she couldn't make him. The knocking at his door continued for another couple of minutes, then he heard Maryann, the innkeeper, mutter a curse word under her breath and turn away from the door. He chuckled to himself. Maryann was a unique woman, and this place was much more than just an inn. It was a large old mansion that had been converted into a hotel—The Harrington Hotel.

Maryann explained to him when he arrived five months ago that the hotel had been in her family for three generations; before that, the mansion was owned by a very wealthy family. Her grandfather claimed he turned it into a hotel so the beauty of the place could be shared with everyone, but Mr. Jones had a different theory. He thought, no, he knew that this house had extraordinary power, like magic. The outside world didn't exist here, and that was precisely the way he wanted it.

The Harrington Hotel had the power to show him his life before that fateful night.

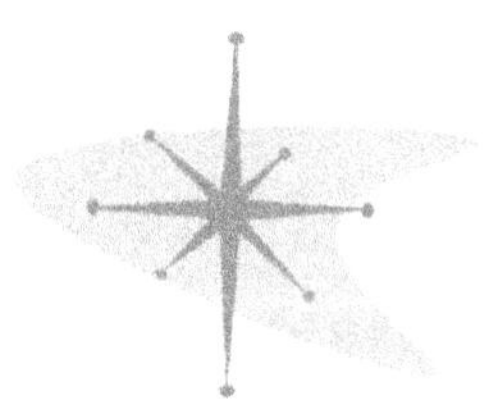

Mark Jones' life changed five months ago, and not for the better. The incident happened the night of his engagement party. He and his fiancé, Cathy, were both from extraordinarily wealthy families, and their lives were perfect. They often joked that they were the golden pair and that nothing terrible would ever touch them. But, boy, were they wrong.

Mark and Cathy's parents donated to the right charities and attended all the right events, and Mark and Cathy followed suit. However, he always thought their support was hollow. Yes, the charities loved getting the money, but he felt they never did enough for those who actually needed the help. Instead, most of the money received went to the organization's executives. He would love to help *the people*, but that is just not how it was done in their circle.

"Mark, you're driving like an old lady. Step on it. We're going to be late for our own engagement party." Cathy laughed as Mark playfully swatted her arm.

"Stop bugging me, Cathy. I'm driving as fast as I can." He laughed as he said this and accelerated just enough, so she didn't complain again about how slow he was driving.

The engagement party was a high-society event at her parent's house, where champagne flowed freely and uniformed staff delivered delicious finger foods to tuxedoed guests. But Mark had a feeling all day that something terrible would happen.

He should have suspected his impending doom based on the weather that night. They watched as their guests ran for cover outside and opened their umbrellas as the clouds pelted out their drops of water. Puddles were splashing as the rainfall became heavier. The roofs of the cars shimmered with spray, and they heard rain splattering outside through the window, which sounded like the buzzing of angry bees.

Her parents begged them to stay overnight, but Cathy insisted they leave. "It's just a little rain." Her defiance toward her parents showed through every time she spoke to them. Instead, she wanted to go back to her house that night. She figured there would be enough togetherness with her family during their high-society week-long wedding next month.

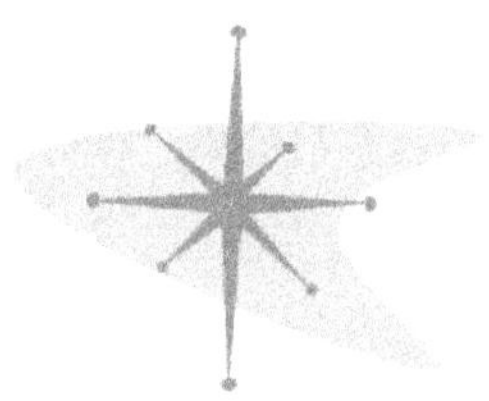

The visibility was terrible, and they had to take a detour through the city because the road out of town was flooded. So Mark took a shortcut he used to take when he worked downtown. He maneuvered his 1953 Jaguar through the narrow alleyway. He was comfortable accelerating because the alley was deserted, so when the man stepped out in front of the car, he was going too fast to stop in time.

The second he heard the thud, he got out of the car.

"Mark, get back into the car. You're getting soaked."

"I am not worried about getting wet, Cathy. I am worried that I killed someone."

"I'm sure he is fine. We will call someone when we get home."

"Cathy, by that time, he could be dead."

"You didn't even hit him that hard. Just leave him, and let's go." They were yelling to be heard over the storm, but Cathy wasn't just yelling for that reason. She was furious that Mark had stopped and that he was concerned about the man. "Get in the car this instance."

Mark knew then that he didn't have a future with Cathy; he would never leave an injured man. So, he defied her instructions and went to take care of the man, leaving her in the car. He brought the man he hit over by the car's headlights and looked at his injuries.

The man was conscious, so Mark tried to get some information from him.

"Sir, can you tell me your name?"

"I'm John." Mark looked into the face of the man he hit and tried to memorize every wrinkle, every mark. This man could be thirty or seventy years old—the full beard and weathered skin made it difficult to tell."

"John, are you okay?"

"Yes, son, I'm fine."

"Let's get you up, and I'll take you to a hotel." The man appeared homeless, and he wasn't going to leave him on the street in this weather.

"Oh no, that's not necessary."

"Oh yes, it is. I want to ensure you are okay."

Mark helped the man into his car.

"You're not bringing him in here, are you? Mark, you don't know what kinds of diseases he has."

"Cathy, be quiet."

"No, I will not be quiet. You can't bring him into this car."

Mark noticed that John winced at Cathy's cruel words.

"Sir, that's okay. You can leave me. I'm fine."

"I will not leave you. I will bring you to a hotel so I know you are in a warm, dry place tonight."

"Thank you, sir, that would be very kind."

"I don't think—"

"Frankly, Cathy, I don't care what you think. I'm going to take care of this gentleman. Then I'll drop you off at home."

"He is not a gentleman," Cathy said under her breath.

"Cathy, that is enough!"

She finally stopped talking while Mark got John in the car. Once Mark dropped him off at the hotel, Cathy was all over him.

"Mark, I can't believe you let that man into our car, and I can't believe you spoke to me in that fashion. What are my parents going to say about this?"

"I don't care what your parents say about this. It was the right thing to do. And if you and your parents are such snobs that you can't have someone like John in your vicinity, then I don't think we should get married."

"What? You have to be kidding me. You would break our engagement, our perfect life, for that bum?"

"He's not a bum. He's a man who had a hard life and is trying to do the best he can. Do you know what he told me, Cathy? He is a veteran, he fought for our country, and you would have me leave him to die in an alley after I hit him with my car?"

"Yes. I can't believe you would consort with such a man. Or that you would throw away our life together for a person that you don't know."

Mark pulled up to Cathy's house. "Cathy, let's table this discussion until tomorrow. Now, I will walk you to the door."

"No, don't bother. I can do it myself." Cathy got out, slammed the car door, and stomped her way up the steps to her house. Mark waited until he knew she was safely inside.

He put his head in his hands and thought, how did I not see what Cathy was like? Then he answered himself—because I was just like her—a snob.

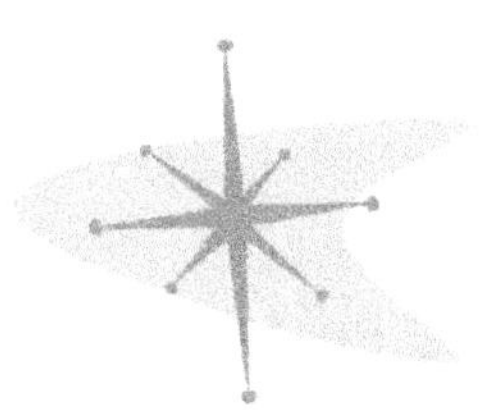

The following day Mark grabbed his newspaper from the front stoop. When he unrolled the paper, the headline read: MAN DIES AT THE HOTEL WHITMORE

"No. It can't be. Mark continued to read the story, and sure enough, it sounded like John. Mark left his name off the registry, having them simply put the name of John.

He couldn't believe that John was dead—he had killed him.

In hindsight, he should've taken John to the hospital, not a five-star hotel. Mark thought he did the right thing, but that wasn't the case. He knew he needed to get away for a couple of days to sort this out in his head. So, he drove and somehow ended up at The Harrington Hotel. He would eventually have to leave someday and face his future, but right now, he knew he was in the right spot.

Maryann encouraged him to relive the events that occurred that night. She wanted the house to show him what happened after he left, but the house wouldn't show Mark until he proved he was ready.

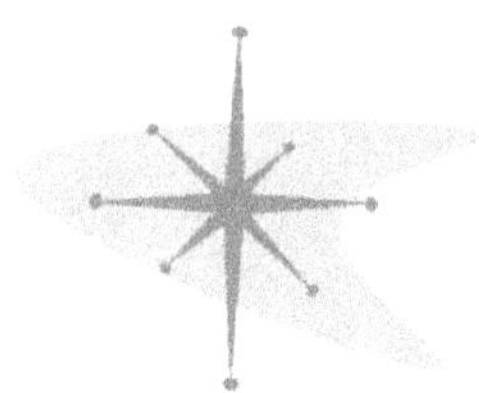

When Mark came to the dining room for dinner, Maryann gently scolded him. "You need to see what happened after you left. Ask the house to show you."

"No, I'm not ready yet. The house won't show me until I say I am ready. You can't make me leave." Mark stomped back up the stairs and to his room.

"No, I can't, but I can move it along," Maryann murmured as Mark sulked away.

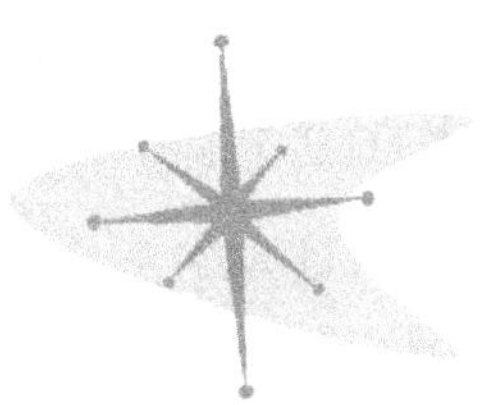

Later that night…

Mark dreamed of his life with Cathy, the fancy parties, the over-the-top lifestyle. He wondered what would become of him without that money. Was he enough of a man on his own?

He woke up in the morning, the sun streaming through the window, and he felt different than he had every other day when he woke up in this room. When he first got here, the things the house could do freaked him out, but after this long, he was used to it and even relished what the house could do for him.

He often spoke to the house, and today was the most important conversation. "House, please show me the night that changed it all, the night I killed John."

The air sparkled. Then he looked at the scene before him—that horrible sight of John's body lying on the pavement. Then the visions continued like a movie showing the rest of the events that he remembered of the evening and ending with him opening the newspaper the following day and seeing the horrible headline.

Then the air sparkled again, and he saw John leaving the hotel room and looking through the alleys, finally finding someone. He saw John talking to a man who looked several years older than him. The man was curled up in a ball, trying to stay warm and dry, but visibly shaking from the cold. John turned him over to look at him and gasped. The man had a blueish tinge to his lips and skin. John knew from living on the streets how serious this could be. He got the man to his feet and dragged him to the hotel room Mark had gotten for him.

Once they stumbled into the room, John attended to the man. He fed, dried, and put him in bed; wrapped him in blankets until the man finally started to warm up. About an hour later, John walked over to the bed, felt for the man's pulse, but found none. He gently closed the man's eyelids.

"Rest in peace, my dear friend." John walked out of the hotel room and back into the stormy night.

Mark was sitting on his bed, not believing what he saw— he didn't kill John. John was still alive, and Mark hid out for months in this strange place like a coward. Well, he was going to leave right now and make this right.

Knock, knock, knock. The sound echoed through the hallway. She was back again.

"Maryann, I'm getting ready to leave. I'll be down in a minute."

"Mark, it's not Maryann. It's Cathy."

He ran to the door and swung it open.

"Cathy, what are you doing here?"

"Looking for you." She walked in and wrapped him up in a fierce hug. "We have been so worried about you."

"Who is we?" As he said this, another person appeared in his doorway. "John, oh my God, I am so glad you are alive."

"I'm so sorry this happened. I never..." John broke down. Mark grabbed him in an embrace, "But how are the two of you together?"

"Well, when I didn't hear from you the next day, my parents and I went to your house. I saw the newspaper lying on the table and surmised that you had left because you thought John had died. So, my parents and I went to the police station. Dad knows someone on the force, and when he showed me a picture of the man who was found dead in the hotel room, I knew it wasn't John. So, we went to the streets to find him, enlisted all our friends' help, and by the end of the day, we tracked John down."

"You did all that?"

"Yes, we did all that. I am so proud of my mom and dad. I never thought that they would step up as they did."

"You organized all of it?"

"Yes, after you dropped me off, I spent the night thinking about how horrible I was to you, both of you, especially John. I was ashamed of myself about the whole situation and decided that I could do better in my life and the lives of others." Mark grabbed her and hugged her tightly.

"You don't know how much this means to me."

"Yes, I think we both do." Cathy looked at John, and they smiled.

"See, we have been looking for you for the last week and have worked together. My parents were offering a huge reward, and we got a lot of bogus tips, but today we finally got an anonymous tip that was good, and they wouldn't take the money. They just wanted to ensure we got here as soon as possible."

Mark smiled, knowing that it was Maryann that called and left the tip.

"I'm glad you found me, but I have been gone for five months. Did you only start looking for me this last week?"

"Maryann explained that you would be a little confused. She said that time moves differently here. You have only been gone a week." Cathy grabbed his hand.

"Wow, this really is an amazing house," Mark said. "So, what now, Cathy?"

"Now we go home, get married, and live our perfect lives together by helping others."

"Sounds perfect to me."

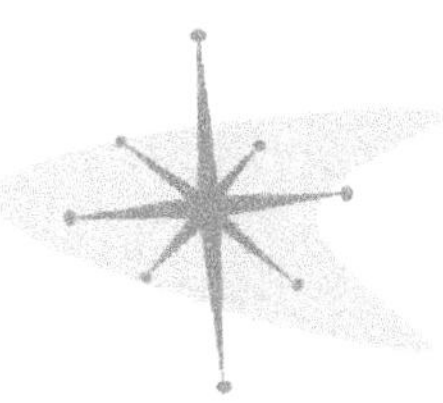

One month later...
"You may kiss the bride."
Mark and Cathy were married in a small private ceremony, where John was the best man. They used the money they saved for the wedding to start the Irving Martin Homeless Foundation in honor of John's friend, the one that died that fateful night.

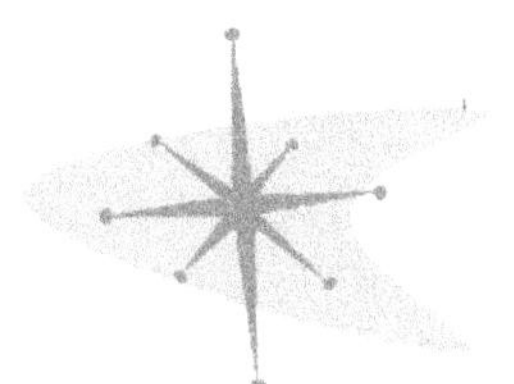

STORY FIVE
The Harrington Hotel
The Origin Story
By Ann Aubitz

Maryann felt a shift in the house's energy the moment she woke. The regular vibration was off, and it seemed as if the house was sad. She knew it sounded crazy that a house could feel emotions, but she truly felt that way. Because she knew that this was no ordinary house—it was magic.

Whenever guests arrived, Maryann explained that The Harrington Hotel had been in her family for three generations; before that, a wealthy family owned the mansion. Her grandfather claimed he turned it into a hotel so the beauty of the place could be shared with everyone, which wasn't exactly the truth. Instead, this was a place where lost souls came to find peace.

"Honey, who's checking in today?" Jim took the steps two at a time to get down to his one true love and wife, Maryann. She was looking at the registry and sighed.

"There are no guests today."

"What do you mean there are no guests today? We have guests every day."

"I know it sounds crazy, but the house feels sad today."

"No, I don't think that sounds crazy at all. Everyone is sad once in a while, and the house has a right to be sad too."

"Oh Jim, that's why I love you. I can say anything, and you'll find a way to explain it."

"Thanks, but why do you think the house is sad, and why don't we have any guests?"

"I don't know. But I feel like something bad is about to happen."

"Honey, I'm sure everything will be fine. The house can take care of itself."

"I'm sure you are right." Those words came out of her mouth, but she wasn't sure everything would be fine.

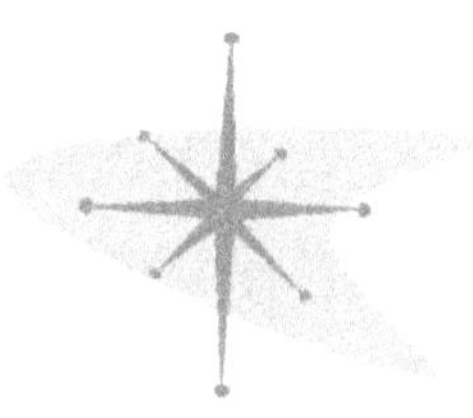

A little later that afternoon...

"Maryann, come quick!"

"What's the matter, Dad?" She was huffing because she ran up the long staircase to get to her father on the second floor.

"Look at the walls; they look like they're bleeding."

"What do you mean bleeding?" She stood beside him and inspected the ornately carved wood decorating the walls. Sure enough, there was a substance that could only be described as blood running down the walls.

"Dad, what is happening?"

"I don't know, honey-bun, but something is very wrong with the house."

"What can we do to help it?"

"I think it best if we all go downstairs in the living room and let the house sort itself out."

"Do you think it will?"

"Only time will tell."

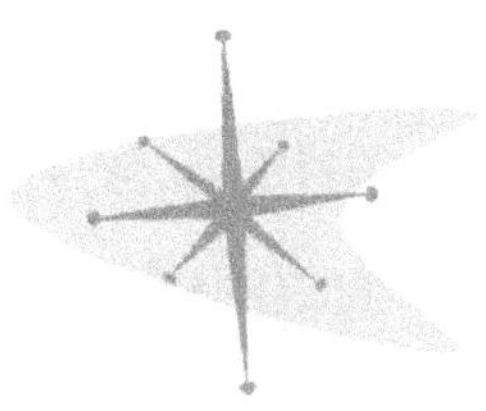

Instead of going to the living room as her father said, Maryann went to the library. She had never wanted to know more about the house's history or where it got its magic. She knew that the house brought people to it who needed help and that was good enough for her. But now she felt that a bit of research would be instrumental in helping her solve the mystery of why the house was behaving so strangely.

She grabbed the oldest book in the library collection, *The History of The Harrington Mansion*. The book was heavy in her hands, so she went to the nearest table, set it down, and started reading. Later, the words began to blur on the page, and she realized by looking at the time on the old grandfather clock that she had been reading for hours.

The stories were just so interesting she couldn't stop reading. Her grandfather put the book together and mentioned that the Harrington family had died. The strange thing was that the story didn't mention how they died, just that they were all gone in one night.

Maryann never knew why the house had magical powers and was able to help lost souls, but she figured it out from the book.

In the late 1800s, The Harrington Mansion was built on a sacred site. The Indigenous peoples of North America had chosen this site as their sacred land. The site released angry spirits that embodied the house when the settlers pushed their people out of this area.

George Harrington built on the land where the sacred site was, even though the native elders told him that the spirits would retaliate. The elders explained that the spirits were here to heal the world's lost souls. That didn't stop George Harrington from building his house on the land. George made his great fortune from the mining industry; he was considered a hardnosed businessman who didn't take no for an answer.

The fateful night that changed everything was said to have been caused by a stranger. He was passing through and camped in the woods that abutted Harrington's land.

Maryann was deep in thought when suddenly, a loud banging sound disrupted her concentration.

"What was that?" she said, running into the living room where her father and husband were seated.

"I don't know, but the house sounds mad."

"I think so too, but why?" They had to shout to be heard over the loud banging sounds coming from the basement.

"I think I've figured out why strange things are happening, but I don't know why they are happening *now*." Maryann saw movement from outside the windows. It looked as if a man was trying to get into the house. "I see someone outside trying to get in. I am going to get them."

"No, Maryann, it could be dangerous."

"It's not dangerous. It's what we have been waiting for to explain what has been going on today."

She ran to the door before Jim or her father could say anything else. She threw open the door as she saw a shadowy figure trying to get out through the fence. It was locked, so he was trying to climb over it."

"Hey you, come here."

"No, I don't want anything to do with this house."

"Please, I think the house needs you."

The stranger stopped trying to climb the fence and turned to face Maryann. She then noticed that his clothes were from long ago and hung in tatters around his body.

"Please, sir, come in. We can take care of you."

"That's what I'm afraid of."

"There is no need to be afraid. The house helps everyone. It brought me my husband, when I was at my loneliest, and it brings people from all over the world to provide clarity in their lives. It can help you too."

"I don't think it wants to."

"I think it does. The house was upset that you were trying to leave. Please come in out of the cold, and we'll give you something warm to drink."

By this time, her father and husband had come to the door to protect Maryann, who never needed protection. Maryann was the one person they could count on that would always do the right thing for others. She never questioned her lot in life and never swayed from the house's mission of helping lost souls.

The man started moving toward the door, and Maryann swore that the house heaved a sigh of relief.

"See, the house wants you here." Maryann stepped aside so the man could enter the foyer. They all looked at each other for a moment, unsure of what to do. Then Maryann remembered her manners.

"I'm sorry, sir, I promised you something hot to drink. Let me get that for you. Please lead him to the sitting room so we can enjoy our tea." She motioned for Jim and her dad to help the stranger find his way to the sitting room. "Wait. I apologize. Where are my manners? My name is Maryann, this is my husband Jim, and my father Mervin, and you are?"

"My name is Zachery Banks." He looked around in fright as if something or someone was going to jump out and attack him.

"I assure you, Zachery, you are safe here." Maryanne put her hand on his arm.

"I'm sorry, ma'am, but you don't know that. You don't know what I have done."

"Well, let me get you some tea, and we'll talk about it. I'm sure it can't be that bad."

They were all seated in the living room enjoying the hot tea when the house moaned again. Zachery jumped out of his seat in panic and headed for the door. A force put him back down in his chair, and there he sat until Maryann started the conversation again.

"So, Zachery, why do you think the house is angry with you?"

"Because of what I did all those years ago." Zachery was on the verge of tears and wiped the water from his eyes with his sleeve. "Because of what I did to the family who lived here."

"The Harringtons?" Maryann knew the story was difficult for him to tell, so she wanted to be as gentle as possible with her next question. "Zachery, what happened to the Harringtons?"

Maryann had searched through all the books she could find in the library, but none of them mentioned what fate had become of the family.

"I-I-I killed them." A shimmering ball of light appeared over the group, and the house shook with energy. "I need to get out of here before it kills me." He tried to no avail to get out of his seat. It was as if something was holding him down.

"Sir, I am sure the house doesn't intend to harm you. On the contrary, it has called you here to help you."

"I don't think that is the case." The man was shaking where he sat as he watched the ball of light float closer and closer to his position in the room. "The house has been calling me back here for years, and until today I was able to stay away. This morning I woke and was in the very place I was on that fateful night sixty years ago."

"What happened?"

"I don't want to talk about it. I want this ball of light to go away."

"I don't think it will until you say what is in your heart."

"I-I-I'm sorry. I never meant for anything bad to happen to your family. Please forgive me."

A blast of energy came out of the ball and zapped the man where he was sitting. It looked like the stream of light electrocuted him, but after a moment, he was okay and looked more at peace than Maryann had ever seen a person look.

"Zachery, are you okay?"

He smiled. "The house has forgiven me. It said I never killed the family that lived here—it wasn't my fault." He was so guilt-ridden because he thought he killed the family that he took his own life, and his spirit retreated to the woods.

Zachery took his own life and never forgave himself, even in death, so he could not pass from this place.

"Will you explain why you thought you killed the family?"

"Yes, the spirits want you to know."

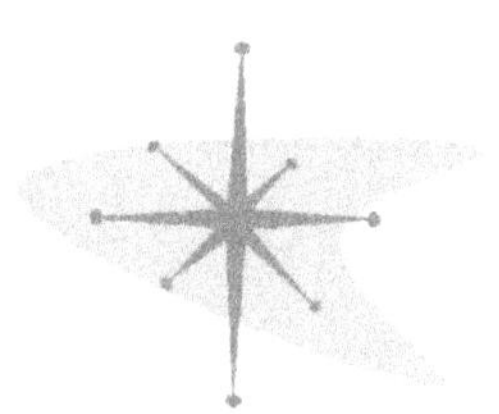

Zachery told the story the best he could…

"The spirits on this sacred site were so upset with George that they made Harrington's life a living hell in the house. Still, George would not move his family. His adult son and new daughter-in-law lived in the house with him, and they just had a baby girl." Zachery had been looking down at his feet as he told the story, but when he got to this part, he looked up at Maryann.

"The spirits spoke through the daughter-in-law asking George to relocate, but he refused. So, the night I camped in the forest, I thought I had left the embers burning, and they caught the house on fire. But it wasn't me." His voice cracked. "It was the spirits. They were punishing the family for building on this land."

"But how could the house have burned down? We are standing in it."

The house shimmered and then reduced itself to the rubble that it was.

Maryann looked around at what was once was a beautiful mansion. "But I don't understand." Tears were running down her face.

"Maryann, you are the grandchild of George Harrington. The spirits wanted his family to help others in a way that George Harrington never did. So, your spirits remained in this place. When Jim died in the forest after the fight with his fiancé, he was allowed to be with you."

"And what now, Zachery? What do the spirits want us to do now?"

"They release you and thank you for all you have done. You are free to go."

Maryann grabbed her father and husband's hands and they disappeared in the cool forest breeze.

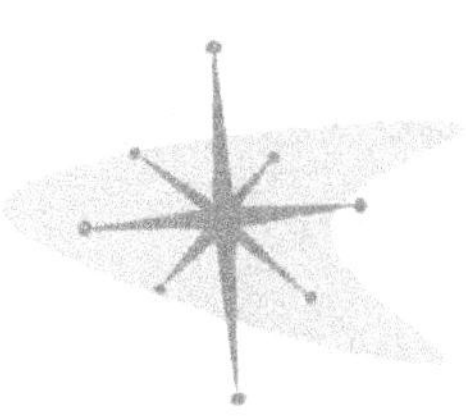

A month later…

Nicholas and Chloé, former guests of The Harrington Hotel, drove through the dense forest for hours but couldn't find the hotel again. They wanted to surprise Maryann and tell her that they got married in Paris and were straightening up his affairs in the United States so they could return to France to run her family's inn. They brought Maryann a gift to show her how much her help meant to them. It was a replica of the Eiffel Tower in a snow globe.

They finally went into town and stopped at the diner for food and directions. The place smelled of fried food and strong black coffee.

"Hello, can I take your order?" The pretty server was young, not more than sixteen.

"Yes, but first, I have a question. Could you please tell us how to get to The Harrington Hotel?"

"No, I am not sure where that is. Let me get Ed. He is old. He'll know." Nicholas put his hand over his mouth to stifle a laugh. He remembered when he was young and thought everyone older was ancient.

"Hello, I heard you were looking for The Harrington Hotel. I haven't heard of a hotel, but there was an old mansion called The Harrington."

"Yes, that must be it. Could you please give us directions? We searched for hours but couldn't find it."

"Well yeah, but it burned down to the ground in the late 1800s, well over sixty years ago."

Chills went up and down Nicholas' spine. "It couldn't be. We were there just two months ago." He looked at Chloé and felt his emotions mirrored in her face.

An older man from the adjoining table spoke up. "I can drive you out that way, but I will only take you as far as the forest surrounding the grounds. Strange things happen if you step foot on the sacred site."

"What do you mean by sacred site? Is the mansion built on a burial site?"

"Not a burial site, but a sacred site. The natives of this area had chosen this site as their sacred land. The site released angry spirits that embodied the house when the settlers pushed their people out. They warned George Harrington not to build his house there, but he wouldn't listen."

They followed the older man in his beat-up 1940 blue pickup truck. He honked as he pointed out the window toward the intense fog. He pulled over to the side of the road and rolled down his window.

"Get out of your car and follow the path up to the wrought iron fence."

"Thank you, sir, you have been a big help."

Nicholas and Chloé stepped gingerly through the fog to avoid disturbing spirits. He felt the same electricity pouring through his body when he stepped into the hotel two months ago. He still held the little snow globe he had bought for Maryann in Paris. It was a peace offering since he wasn't all that nice to her when they first met.

Chloé turned to him. "It will be okay."

"Why do you say that?"

"Because you are shaking."

"Yes, it is a little unnerving, isn't it?"

"Yes, it is. It's as if a current is running through my body. I felt the same way when I stepped into the hotel's foyer two months ago."

"So did I." Nicholas agreed.

They walked in silence up the steep path to the clearing. The gate didn't open for him this time, so they stood and stared at the destruction in front of them. The house was burned to the ground. There were a few outlines of rooms left, but for the most part, it was rubble and ash. They could tell that it had been this way for some time. He bent down and placed the snow globe in front of the gate.

"Maryann, this is for you, you changed my life, and I thank you."

"Both of our lives," Chloé added.

"Both of our lives." He repeated as he grabbed his wife's hand and turned to walk away. Just as they stepped away from the gate, it began to open.

"What do you say, should we go in?"

"Well, we've come this far."

They walked together hand in hand to what would have been the foyer and the check-in desk. Part of it remained, although it was covered with moss and other nature. Nicholas walked behind it and stood in the very place that Maryann stood when she greeted him for the first time. He glanced down at his feet and saw the registry book sticking out from under some rubble. A new shiver went through his body. His name was on the last sheet of the registry, along with Chloé's. Dropping the book, he grabbed her hand and ran toward the car.

"Are you going to tell me what you saw?" Chloé gasped for breath as she slid into the car's front seat.

"I saw our names on the registry."

"You what?"

"I saw our names on the registry. We were at this very spot two months ago. It was magic that brought us back together." Nicholas looked freaked out, but Chloé was as cool as a cucumber.

"And I will thank that magic daily for the rest of our lives." Chloé smiled and grabbed his hand.

They drove away and cherished their second chance together because of the magical spirits at The Harrington Hotel.

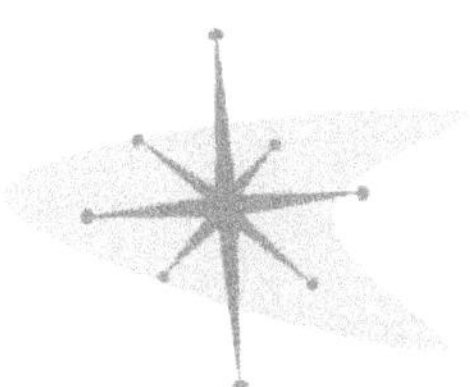

About the Author

Ann Aubitz is the co-owner and publisher of Kirk House Publishers and FuzionPress, located in Burnsville, Minnesota. After years of reading everything she could get her hands on, she decided to help others achieve their dream of becoming an author. Her mission is to help authors reach their goals by seeing their books in print.

Ann is also a proud member of the Independent Book Publishers Association, a board member-at-large for the Midwest Independent Publishers Association, and a group leader for Women of Words (WOW). She also chairs the yearly WOW writing conference.

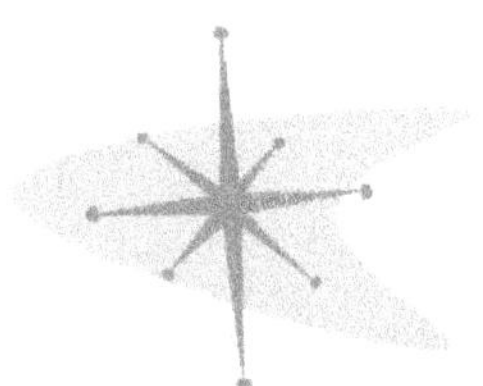

STORY SIX
The Old Bennett Place
By Leandra Logan

Joanie Ames surveyed the room, lively with partygoers. Her dream of pledging to the Omega Phi Delta Sorority was a whiff away!

This last tea of 1964 was being held at the sorority house to present the chosen pledges to Omega's current members and alums.

Ladies, young and old, mingled as hired classmen circulated with cakes and canapes. It was a picture Joanie wanted to remember for the rest of her life: a pastel watercolor, with its muted swirl of fancy shirtwaist dresses and white dinner jackets.

Joanie's dress was pale green chiffon. She'd worked at Woolworth's soda fountain all summer to fund her sorority rush. Finally, it was paying off, for she looked like she truly belonged!

Joanie patted her cap of golden hair adorned with a silver butterfly barrette. Truth be told, most of the butterflies fluttered around her stomach due to last-minute jitters. But Joanie was determined not to show it.

Just then, her sister Rosemary caught her eye. Rosemary was an Omega member of good standing. Now twenty-six, Rosemary worked downtown as a paralegal for a law firm. Mom and Dad were so proud of her! Joanie wanted a piece of that action. Despite their eight-year age difference, she and Rosemary looked very much alike, and Joanie had long tried to match Rosemary in everything from grades to bubbly personality.

Rosemary favored her sister with a wink, then turned back to her sorority sisters. Joanie understood her distance. It was up to Joanie to bravely step forward at these functions, circulate and make a good impression. Then it was up to her to excel at college studies, graduate, and find a splendid job—a job downtown with any luck!

Sorority connections were supposed to help career girls succeed. A practical reason beyond the joys of belonging to a loyal sisterhood, making lifelong friends, and living in a beautiful campus house for the next four years as she attended classes.

Joanie's toes tingled in her snug high heels as she approached a linen-covered table boasting a cut glass bowl full of orange sherbet punch, matching cups, and silver trays full of finger food. She carefully ladled the punch and filled a cup without spilling.

Five other pledges made the final cut like Joanie, and two now joined her for punch. The taller of the two haughtily lifted her chin, caressed some pricy pearls at her throat, and twirled away to speak to sorority president Gretchen Talbot. The shorter, plumper girl, Denise, gazed shyly at Joanie. Denise wasn't the colorful personality sororities typically rushed, but Denise was a genius and her aunt a celebrated alumna.

"Almost in." Denise watched the guests from behind her cat's-eye glasses.

Joanie sipped her punch. "Except for the final Halloween initiation tomorrow."

Denise visibly shuddered beneath her tight pink dotted-Swiss dress. "My auntie naturally upholds the Omega sisterhood code of secrecy, but she seems worried about me. Unfortunately, she couldn't make it today."

"When did your aunt graduate, Denise?"

"Only five years ago. Which suggests our initiation is likely similar, if not identical to hers."

"My sister," Joanie said, pointing to Rosemary, "graduated four years ago."

"Does she seem concerned for you?"

"I haven't seen much of her lately. She has her own apartment."

Denise sighed. "Good luck to us."

Joanie nodded solemnly.

Joanie awoke Halloween morning to discover Rosemary at the kitchen table for a change. Joanie grabbed a cup of coffee and sat beside her while their mother flipped hotcakes at the stove.

"Big day!" Rosemary rejoiced as Mom served Joanie hotcakes.

Joanie's eyes forlornly dropped to her plate.

Rosemary patted Joanie's hand on the table. "I know you're worried about tonight's final initiation, but it'll be a breeze. Honestly!"

"Blah, blah, sorority secrecy! Can't you help even a little bit, Rose?"

Rosemary grew thoughtful. "I suppose it wouldn't be letting the cat out of the bag to say the odds are with you— the way the initiation *activities* are set up."

"Huh?"

"Joanie! Read between the lines! The odds are *against* you being scared out of your wits. And that's probably even more than I should've revealed." Rosemary kissed her cheek, leaving a lipstick smudge. "Must scoot to catch my bus downtown. Talk tomorrow."

"When it's over," Joanie finished glumly.

"At which time, you will be inducted into Omega Phi Delta!"

The six pledges met at the sorority house at seven o'clock that evening to join the sisters in residence. Everyone was wearing mandatory dungarees and dark hooded sweatshirts. Sorority president, Gretchen, silenced the commotion with a brisk clap.

"Welcome pledges to the final challenge on your path to Omega sisterhood." She raised a clear glass vase containing folded paper squares. "In this vessel, I hold the tasks to be performed this All Hallows Eve. You will draw a paper and execute the task written on it. Some challenges are easier than others. But that is the spice of life. As we move forward, we will face many such games of chance. Handling them well will only strengthen us." Gretchen shook the vase to make the papers bounce. "Come line up, and tempt fate."

A redhead reached into the jar. She nervously unfolded her white square of paper, then sighed in relief.

"Read your task to us," Gretchen instructed.

"Wax four storefront windows along Division Avenue."

A raven-haired foreign exchange student stepped up next. "Dress like a baby," she read, "and trick-or-treat with a sorority sister."

Like Joanie, the remaining pledges didn't appear especially happy for the pair. Four tasks remained, at least one of which certainly wasn't going to be a cinch.

Two more pledges drew tasks.

"Ring the college dean's doorbell repeatedly at one a.m."

"Hang a frat boy's underpants from the flagpole on the quad."

Joanie glanced at her friend, Denise. They each dug into the jar for the remaining slips of paper.

"Spend the hours of eight till midnight in the Bennett mansion!" Denise lamented. "Four whole hours with that family of ghosts?"

The pledges gasped in dismay. Everyone in the small college town knew of the house on Larkspur Lane where the family of six had perished in a Halloween fire eight years ago. The firemen had managed to quash the flames quickly, but smoke inhalation had already taken them.

It was also widely known that the college clock two blocks away was chiming twelve when the firemen reached the victims, expired in their beds. Which was a shock, as the men reported seeing children in costume flitting room to room as they stormed in, calling for survivors.

Since then, rumors had besieged the college town each Halloween of passersby glimpsing flitting figures behind the windowpanes.

Joanie guiltily felt a ripple of relief. That had to be the worst task. She then opened her slip of paper. "Spend the hours of eight till midnight in the Bennett mansion." She repeated the identical instructions dully.

"Chop-chop ladies," Gretchen sang out. "You will find necessary equipment in the kitchen, such as furniture polish and brushes for the window painting, a key to the boys' locker room to fetch those skivvies for the flagpole, baby clothes for trick-or-treating."

The girls got moving, some giving Joanie and Denise consolatory pats.

Gretchen personally escorted Joanie and Denise to the former Bennett residence. Streetlights glowed in the gathering darkness as they marched through the grand old neighborhood full of majestic homes built at the turn of the century. Costumed children, their shell-like masks bobbing, darted everywhere, gripping precious candy sacks.

The trio paused before the well-known mansion on a corner lot, surrounded by black iron fencing. The Victorian was in sad disrepair with peeling blue paint and loose white shutters. Yet, though dirty, its window panes still somehow managed to catch the moon's eerie glow.

Gretchen pushed open the gate, which gave an ominous creak. Joanie and Denise followed her up the cracked sidewalk.

As they climbed the sagging porch steps, Denise commented, "I wonder what it's like on the inside."

Gretchen flashed her a superior smile. "It's not bad. Flames scorched the interior, but things just look and smell like they've been partially barbecued. The furniture, for instance, is streaked black but intact. The grandmother inherited the place, but apparently, lives frozen in despair and disbelief, refusing to enter it, much less sell it."

"Poor Grandma," Denise murmured.

Joanie noted with surprise that Gretchen spoke with authority, as if, at some point, she'd personally been in the place. And *she* certainly didn't seem fearful.

"I won't give anything more away," Gretchen continued. "You'll be finding out all about it firsthand. And I don't mean standing by the front windows for four hours. You'll be exploring the house from top to bottom."

"You can't be serious!" Denise cried.

"You must collect the dozen small plastic jack-o-lanterns planted in the rooms. When finished, wait inside until the tower clock chimes twelve. I'll be back here by then on the porch waiting."

"You're leaving us here alone?" Denise demanded.

"I'm no nursemaid. Oh, c'mon, it's not that bad," Gretchen consoled. "As sorority president, it was my duty to hide the pumpkins myself yesterday, and I'm still in one piece."

"Hid them in the daytime, I bet," Denise grumbled.

"Long before the Bennett family's annual witching hour," Joanie added.

An unrepentant Gretchen moved along the porch and pushed open a window. "This is how you'll enter. There is a sofa on the other side of the sill to break your fall, but beware, it is grimy."

"You promised flashlights," Joanie grumbled.

Gretchen reached into her daisy-figured tote bag and produced them. "And here is a pillowcase to stash the little jack-o-lanterns. Now in you go."

The girls gingerly climbed over the sill and bounced onto the sofa. The air inside the house proved stale, moist, and smoky, causing them to gag. They jumped as Gretchen pushed the window firmly back into place, sealing them inside.

Moonlight provided faint illumination. Joanie slowly pivoted to take in her surroundings. It seemed this room was the library, with shelves of books lining the walls, a rolltop desk in a corner, and sadly, an abandoned children's desk near a rack of yellow-spined Nancy Drew mysteries.

Denise lingered beside Joanie, swinging her flashlight beam. "I am so scared!" she whimpered. "Turn on your light too."

"No." Joanie instead stuffed the small cylinder in the pouch of her sweatshirt. "It's a mistake to wear down both sets of batteries simultaneously. I'll bet some pledges lived to regret it."

"You are so smart, kiddo."

"If we keep calm, Denise, we'll make the best decisions. We've got to prove to the Omegas that we are savvy enough to join them."

"But is it worth this hullabaloo?"

"Of course! My sister and your aunt are rooting for us because they know it's worthwhile to be part of the sisterhood." Joanie clutched the pillowcase. "Let's collect those jack-o-lanterns quickly and come back here to camp until midnight."

Joanie ventured into the hallway while Denise aimed the beam in their path.

They moved on to the living room. It also faced the street, so like in the library, shadows danced along the streaks of moonlight, and the headlights of passing cars burst through the filmy curtains like camera flashbulbs.

Peering outside, they briefly watched the children cruising the sidewalk in their Halloween costumes. Several lingered in front of the Bennett place, some daring to come halfway up the walk, others halting at the boulevard. The closest ones suddenly pointed, hollered, and dashed back to the street.

Denise matched their panic.

"Take it easy," Joanie comforted. "Those kids didn't see any ghost. They must've glimpsed *our* silhouettes!"

"Silly old me." Denise drew a breath. "Any sign of a jack-o-lantern?"

Joanie spied a blob of orange near the boxy television set. "Here's one stashed behind the TV." She squatted to retrieve the hollow toy and toss it in the pillowcase. "Gretchen certainly worked to conceal them."

Cautiously, they moved into the kitchen. It was a large room with kettles on the stove and dishes on the table. "I suppose Mrs. Bennett was too busy with Halloween all those years ago to worry about cleaning up after dinner," Joanie noted. It was as if the family was gone in a puff of smoke, leaving everyday living behind.

It took some searching, but they found a plastic pumpkin inside the encrusted oven.

The girls made progress, finding six jack-o-lanterns on the main level. It was extra tricky because Joanie soon realized that to collect the full dozen, there had to be multiple pumpkins in some areas.

Guardedly, they approached the staircase in the foyer. The other six pumpkins had to be on the second level. Joanie ascended, with Denise gripping both the flashlight and the hem of Joanie's hooded sweatshirt. The beam bounced shakily against the wall, highlighting family photos of the

Bennetts doing everyday things. The girls swiftly averted their eyes from the happy images.

The bedrooms were in disarray like the kitchen was, with belongings scattered as if everyone expected to awaken on November first, 1956.

Ultimately, they peered into the last bedroom facing the rear of the house. It was decidedly masculine, with trophies on a shelf, a writing desk stacked with magazines, and an open notebook ready for homework.

"We are missing three pumpkins," Denise fretted. "And we're out of rooms to search."

Anxious to get back downstairs to wait in the library, Joanie dived in to explore. That was when she saw the figure hovering by the window curtain and let out a scream.

"Hey, pipe down," a young male voice commanded.

"Wha…" Joanie exhaled like a squeaky balloon.

"You're here for an initiation, right?"

"Right," Denise said cautiously.

"Well, I'm on an initiation mission too. I'm Biff."

"I'm Joanie, and this is Denise." He looked harmless enough, Joanie decided, in dungarees and a gray sweatshirt. The right age for a similar fraternity challenge.

"Found your jack-o-lanterns in the dresser."

"You were eavesdropping," Denise accused.

"Sure I was. You could've been anybody."

Joanie delightedly found the last pumpkins. "Have you seen any ghosts yet, Biff?"

"Naw. The Bennetts died eight years ago, after all. Plainly, they moved on to their Heavenly reward."

"You seem so sure."

"You can be too." Biff beckoned the girls closer and stepped back as they joined him. "Look outside without standing in front of the window."

The girls gazed down to find several goblins and witches creeping through the backyard.

"Larger than kids, smaller than guys," Biff prompted.

"The Omegas! Coming to spook us!" Joanie hissed in disgust. "So they *know* there are no ghosts."

"This must be the sisterhood's scam every year," Denise deduced, "to play off the rumors surrounding this house—to give their pledges a big scare!"

Biff chuckled. "Suddenly, you've got the drop on *them*. What are you gonna do about it?"

"Play along and act scared?" Denise suggested.

Joanie scowled. "Hah! Omegas aren't chicken. We need to fight back. But how?"

"Haunt them," Biff suggested. "I found some white sheets in the hall closet, ready in case I need to go Casper, myself."

"Perfect! Hurry, Denise."

"Good luck."

"Ditto, Biff. And thanks."

The girls raided the closet, wrapped musty sheets around them like cloaks, and waited for telltale sounds below. As they heard movement in the foyer, they began to moan and stomp along the upper landing, leaning over the railing with sheets billowing.

The sisters wailed in alarm, fumbled with the front door lock, and burst outside.

When Gretchen returned shortly after midnight, Joanie and Denise were innocently waiting at the library window with a sack full of jack-o-lanterns. Neither party referred to the chaotic happening.

A ceremony soon welcomed Joanie, Denise, and the four others into Omega Phi Delta.

Afterward, Joanie's sister Rosemary took her out for a celebratory milkshake at the Hangout on campus. Joanie regaled her adventure at the Bennett place.

"I thought Biff might be there to help, but I couldn't warn you without breaking the sisterhood oath."

Joanie gaped. "You know about Biff?"

Rosemary smiled faintly. "Biff is a Bennett."

"He's a ghost?"

"He's my ghost, in a way." Rosemary opened her wallet and showed her a photo of Biff and herself in prom attire. "We dated briefly junior year."

"Is he the boy who dumped you after prom?"

"Yes. You were too young to confide in then, but it was hard. Anyway, the fire happened our senior year. Then the following year, I was in Biff's abandoned house for my initiation, feeling sad and terrified, reliving his loss. Luckily, he got Heavenly permission to come back and guide me through it. I wasn't half as brave or clever as you. I merely hid while the sisters hunted for me in costume. It was Biff who drove them off with some moans and thumps."

"Does he come every year to help the pledges?"

"No. Biff likely cashed in a second favor Upstairs to help out my baby sister."

"Maybe he regretted dumping you, Rose."

"Yes, he said so that night. Helping me out was his chance to make amends. We talked for hours. I can only imagine how much he continues to worry about his grandma hanging on to the property. He can only appear in the house, so he can't reach out to her."

Joanie grinned. "Maybe we can repay him by changing all that."

The following week, the Omegas were back at the Bennett place with old Mrs. Bennett. Joanie and Rosemary had convinced her to tour the house and allow the sorority to help her sort it out for resale or demolition.

Afterward, outside, Mrs. Bennett fiercely hugged Joanie and Rosemary. "I am so grateful for the chance to move on."

"Your children want you to," Rosemary assured.

"Yes. It may sound silly, but I thought I spied Biff on the stairs, nodding his head and blowing me a kiss."

"Nothing silly about that!" Joanie chirped. "We never lose our loved ones."

About the Author

Mary Jane Schultz often writes under the penname **Leandra Logan**. She is a multi-published, bestselling author in various genres, including romance, mystery, young adult, and illustrated books for children. Mary Jane is a Romantic Times Awards winner and has received numerous nominations within the industry. Her critics praise her for her deeply emotional stories, often lightened with humor, and the red herrings she thoroughly enjoys planting to keep her readers guessing.

Mary Jane resides in the historic town of Stillwater, Minnesota.

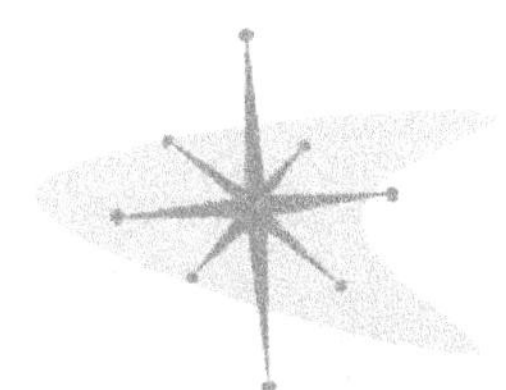

STORY SEVEN
The Spirit World of Indonesia's Mystical Culture
By Gloria VanDemmeltraadt

as told by a young teen-age boy

Many mythical beings have a role in Indonesian mythology. When other beliefs came to the Indonesian archipelago, additional devils, angels, and demons were added to the mix. Belief in local spirits such as the forest guardian, the ghost of water or haunted places still exists, often associated with a spiritual creature, or the tormented soul of a deceased human.

Life in the United States, a younger society that is based on beliefs of love and kindness, is a completely different experience than everyday life in the environment where I grew up. Even though we were a Christian family with Christian friends and acquaintances, the overpowering culture was mystical. Living in a country with ancient roots and thousands of years of supernatural and sorcerous practices taught me first-hand that you don't mess with Indonesia's mystical culture. This shadowy culture is physically and spiritually evident, daily, and there is no denying its presence. Some of my own experiences are told here and they are but an insignificant few of the many paranormal events that take place continually in daily life in Indonesia.

Bird of death

The piet-van-vliet (pronounced pete-von-fleet) is a common bird found in Indonesia, the Philippines, southern China and other nearby areas. It is a small wailing cuckoo. The name, piet-van-vliet, is the sound of the bird's call. The bird is a brood parasite, which means the female lays her eggs in the nests of various other small birds instead of building her own. The belief in Indonesia is that when the piet-van-vliet sings from a tree in your yard, that someone will die very soon in that house. This causes anyone who hears the cuckoo's call to look carefully to see from where the sound is coming.

I have heard the bird calling many times in my youth, but only once was it wailing from a tree in our yard. Sadly, it was the day my beloved caretaker and nanny unexpectedly died.

Voodoo

Voodoo magic, with what they call black magic and the white magic that counteracts certain activities, has been practiced in Indonesia for centuries. As an example, one of my cousins suddenly took sick, developed a fever, and quickly got sicker and sicker over several days. A regular doctor was called in and could find nothing wrong. The family called a "white magic doctor," who discovered under my cousin's mattress, a bunch of herbs and spices wrapped in a banana leaf and speared with bamboo pins. He removed the poisonous ball, her bedding was cleaned, and she immediately recovered. They never found out who put the malicious concoction there, but this was certainly evidence of the practice of black magic.

My mother and her brother were once with a group of young people on holiday from school or work and they were all staying at my grandparents' home. The group went for a walk in the afternoon through the rice fields. As they were about to enter a forest, an old man unexpectedly appeared in the middle of their path. He told them not to go into the forest because it was sacred ground and inhabited by spirits. With this tantalizing warning, the young people couldn't possibly keep from going into the forest. They disregarded the old man, who disappeared as suddenly as he had appeared, and sauntered through the forest enjoying the breeze through the trees and nothing strange seemed to happen. At the other end of the forest, they looked up a steep hill and saw a road with some traffic. When they saw a car coming by, one of them suggested that it would be fun to pretend to cry for help and see what the people would do. They loudly yelled "Help!" and the car stopped. People got out of the car to see what was going on. The young folks hid and laughed when the people searched and called out. Finally, the people went back to their car and drove on.

The kids went back to my grandparents' house, ate dinner and went to bed. During the night one of the girls from the group became ill with a high fever. The others woke up and tried to keep her in bed but she kept on wanting to get up and go outside. She said there was a handsome man outside who was calling her to join him. By this time everyone in the house was awake and they tried to call a doctor for the girl, but the phone wouldn't work. They then decided to take her to the doctor, but their car wouldn't start, nor would any other cars at the house.

The girl was Roman Catholic so they decided to pray. One boy was a spiritually strong person and wanted to pray with the girl's own rosary. They looked in her purse where she always kept her rosary, but no one could find it. All the while, the girl was fighting to get outside to reach the handsome man who she believed wanted to talk to her. No one else saw or heard anything outside.

Not having the rosary, the boy decided to read to her from the Bible to try to calm her down. The girl wouldn't let him read and kept saying that the man outside had a better book and wanted her to join him. The boy instead started to pray the Lord's Prayer with the girl, and as soon as he began, she got very agitated. She was now struggling to get out of the bed, but the others were holding her down. He tried to get her to say the words after him, but she didn't want to do it. He fought with her and struggled for a long time. Finally, in a belligerent voice, she growled, "Our Father!" She made horrible faces and grimaces and after a long while, she said, "Who art in heaven," with more grimaces. Then she said really fast, "Hallowed be thy name!"

Suddenly she looked up at the boy and yelled, "Watch out!" The girl ducked and said, "There's someone up there with a long spear pointed at you!" He kept praying in a loud voice, and the girl cried out that there was an angel who intercepted the attack. She ducked and bobbed around for several minutes, and suddenly the girl calmed down completely. She stretched out on the bed and finished saying the prayer to the end, and promptly fell asleep.

Meanwhile, during the melee, the grandmother in the house had sent a servant to the local native village for a voodoo doctor to come. The voodoo doctor did come and sat by the girl and apparently was listening to the spirit while she was struggling. He asked the group if they had gone into the forest and called for help as a prank. The young people admitted they had and apologized profusely.

After the interception of the attack by the spirit and when the girl had calmed down, the voodoo doctor shook his head and told them the spirit was satisfied for now, but not to do anything like that ever again. He left when the girl was peacefully sleeping, so the rest of them went to bed also. The next morning everyone was well. In addition, the telephone worked, the cars started, and the lost rosary was found in the girl's purse.

Superstition follows both fact and fantasy in most cultures. Indonesia abounds with mystical happenings and whether fantasy or fact, my own experiences have taught me great respect for the paranormal. I describe below several mystical events that helped to reinforce that respect.

Strange things

Strange things began to happen soon after we moved to a specific house in the city of Bandung on the island of Java. It's difficult for me to talk about even today, because others might not understand how strange and just plain creepy some of these events were.

My first recognition of something odd was to see dark shadows. I would be walking in the house, or sitting quietly doing my homework, and suddenly a black shadow would flit by the corner of my eye. Along with this was a dark and heavy feeling. I'd quickly turn my head and nothing would be there. At first, I thought this might be something in my eye, an eyelash or piece of dust or something, but it wasn't. I was really seeing something for a fleeting moment; something black and sinister.

Then I started to hear music. At night, in bed, I would suddenly begin to hear complete symphonies reverberating in my head. We had no radio and there was no way I could be hearing music coming from another source; the neighbors were too far away. This experience was quite pleasant, if odd. I loved music and when I got over my surprise at hearing it, the beautiful music would often lull me to sleep. I was the only one who heard these beautiful concerts, and often thought that if I was a composer, I could become famous by writing down the melodies. This experience lasted off and on for the whole time we lived in that house.

My room on the second floor had a window to the back of the house where there was a stone staircase. The steps led up to a covered walkway and a balcony and a door to the house.

Beneath the balcony was a storeroom. The second-floor bathroom where I showered was near that doorway. I remember several incidents when after I showered and went back to my room, I had a strong feeling that I was being watched. There was never anything or anyone on the walkway outside, but I couldn't shake the feeling that someone was watching me. One day a maid found a snake in my bathroom, which was odd. Snakes don't like cold and it would be abnormal for one to climb the cold stone steps outside. We never found out how that snake got in there, but it was removed and after that I didn't have the feelings of being watched.

One evening I went into my room and turned on the light, and suddenly a hazy ball appeared in the middle of the room. The ball immediately exploded and a curl of white smoke spread over the room. I screamed and within two jumps I was downstairs and in my mother's arms. She could see something had happened and when I told her about the smoke, she said, "It's too bad you didn't catch it!" As I learned later, smoke is a common occurrence with spirits. It is said that if you instantly catch the smoke in a jar and clap on the lid, you have captured the evil spirit and it can no longer hurt you. Fortunately, this never happened to me again, as I can't say I'm in the habit of carrying a jar everywhere I go.

Premonitions

About this time, I began to have unsettling premonitions. Entire scenes would play in my head with people moving and talking and things happening, and I knew with complete certainty that these scenes were really going to happen. One example is going with my dad to Jakarta to the General Motors assembly plant. Waiting for him there, my brother and I were outside looking around. In a village square with grass and trees, a car started to back up into the street on the other side of the grassy square. Out of nowhere I knew exactly what was going to happen. I could see in my mind that a truck would come around the corner and there would be a traffic jam. I knew the drivers would hang out of their windows and talk to each other and I knew that the car would go first, and the truck would then go back into the street and its brakes would squeak loudly. It was a simple and innocent scene; no one got hurt or anything and there was no damage, but I could see the whole thing happening in my mind in color, all before it happened.

After that scene I had other similar premonitions, but they got more menacing each time. One strange forewarning was sometime in 1949. One normal evening on my way to bed upstairs, I placed my foot on the first step, and abruptly, I froze. I was completely stopped from going any farther, and I absolutely could not move my foot to the next step. I suddenly had what can only be called an insight – a message from somewhere that something terrible was going to happen – not at that time, but I knew it would be in the middle of the night. I heard in my mind exactly what was going to happen and knew I would be awakened by a terrible rattling. I can hear the sound now in my mind, as I heard it with my foot on that first step so long ago; a choking sound from something or someone in a desperate death battle. The feeling was strong enough to stop my path up the stairs, but apparently not strong enough for me to tell anyone else about it. I finally overcame the blockage of my steps, and thinking I was imagining things, went on up to bed.

At two o'clock in the morning I was awakened by exactly the sound I had heard in my mind earlier in the evening. It was a horrible, loud, strangled sound made by something that seemed to be choking. The sound came from outside, and I leaped out of bed. With quivering legs, I went to the window, grabbing a sword on the way. I was ready for action!

The terrible sound woke everyone else in our house as well, and the neighbors, too. People were soon milling about looking for the source of the screaming. It turned out the neighbors' dog had tried to jump the four-foot fence into our yard. He was on a leash and the chain was too short to reach over the fence, causing the dog to hang in mid-air. His strangled screams split the night as if it had been cut by my sword.

Before long, the neighbors rescued their dog, which did live through the adventure, although he must have had a very sore throat for a few days, and everyone went back to bed.

These situations began to frighten me and I finally had enough of this. I didn't like the feelings I had when these premonitions came over me and the feelings got more and more unsettling. One day I threw up my hands and yelled out loud, "That's enough – I'm through with you – be gone!" And that was the end of them. It was like something passed out of me – away from me – and I never had another premonition again.

Dogs in the corner

Another event that involved our dogs wasn't really a premonition, but a strange event nonetheless. Our five dogs included a mother with four of her offspring, older than pups. They were some sort of cocker spaniel mix, certainly not the brightest of beasts, but protective of us, and much treasured by all. All were "people" dogs who loved to drape themselves wherever we happened to be. One dark evening the dogs were lying on the floor between the open door to the terrace and the dining table where my mother and I were sitting while she helped with my school work.

Suddenly the entire gang of five bounded up at the same time as if awakened from a terrifying nightmare. Neck hair up, legs and ears stiff, grunting and trembling, almost screaming in their growls, they formed a semi-circle and approached the corner of the room near the rear door. They approached as one and suddenly backed up, obviously very afraid of something in that corner. My shouts to calm them were not heard. I suspected a scorpion or snake or something, and I first looked on the terrace and there was nothing there, nor was there anything to see in the corner. The dogs kept up their crying and now feeling a little anxious, I crept closer. I saw or smelled nothing but suddenly seemed to have the same frightening feeling as the dogs. The hair on my arms rose and the closer I got to the corner, the more I sensed the presence of something dark and fearsome. I heard my mother utter a sound – perhaps a prayer, something she was good at doing – and the entire scene lasted only a few moments. Almost as suddenly as it began, it stopped. Like snow melting in the sun, the anxious feelings disappeared. The dogs calmed and laid down to continue their snoozing and everything went back to normal.

The faith healer

During the time we lived in this house, my parents were having marital difficulties. Also, my mother was having continual problems with asthma, which was not yet fully understood by the medical community. I have never in my life seen anyone have such severe attacks of asthma and she had many hospital stays for breathing problems.

No doubt my mother tried everything she possibly could to get relief from her asthma. A local man was recommended to her by some friends, and I expect that she was desperate to try anything. The man was a sort of doctor, but more of a faith healer. My understanding is that he did not touch her in his treatments; instead, he held his hands high over her and moved from her head to her feet and then shook his hands out. Later she said that she could feel something like prickling needles throughout her body as his hands moved. At first, she had some good results from these treatments and she continued to go to the man's house and sometimes he came to our home.

One thing he did was to determine whether there were "harmful earth rays" in our house. He came to the house to make sure that all of our beds and furniture were correctly positioned. If they were not as he specified, he moved the furniture himself, especially the beds, to align them with the proper earth rays.

One day I was asked to deliver something to this man's house. While I was there, he asked me if I wanted to see a picture of the devil. Being a young teenager, of course I was curious and wanted to see it. He showed me a black and white photograph of an indoor room with furniture and a vague background. Then he showed me another picture with the same background but swirling in the middle of the picture was a curl of white smoke. It didn't look like much to me, and I thought this was nonsense, but he said that it was the devil.

Interestingly, not long after I saw the picture, was the event in my bedroom when I turned on the light and there was the floating fuzzy ball in the middle of the room. That occurrence by itself would have been frightening, but having seen the picture previously, it was terrifying.

Looking back now, I am stunned at the level of trust we had in this man, who was strange to say the least. It was during his treatment of my mother over a couple of years, that many of the abnormal events I have talked about occurred. I have my suspicions as to who or what caused them, but we will never know for sure. Several things happened in a relatively short time to confuse everything, one being that my father left the house. He had been having a relationship with another woman whom he eventually married many years later, and about the end of 1950, he moved out. About the same time, the rest of us moved away from that house, also.

The last event a short time later was that the faith healer passed away. We never found out how or why, but a member of his family came to our house to say he had suddenly died. After this news and the move away from the strange house, the supernatural events that seemed to be plaguing our family abruptly stopped and never reoccurred as long as we lived in that country; a most welcome condition.

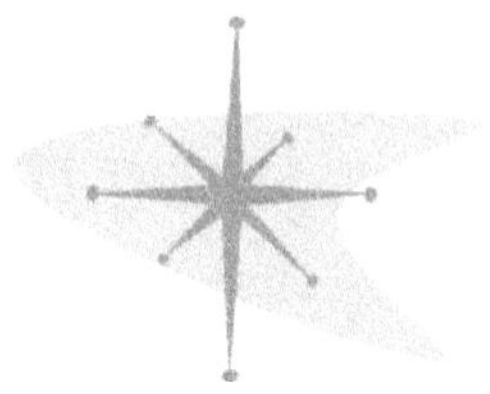

About the Author

Gloria VanDemmeltraadt
Much of her work focuses on drawing out precious memories. As a hospice volunteer, she continues to hone her gift for capturing life stories and has documented the lives of dozens of patients. She refined this gift in *Memories of Lake Elmo*, a collection of remembrances telling the evolving story of a charming village. She continues her passion and has caught the essence of her husband's early life in war-torn Indonesia. In *Darkness in Paradise*, Onno VanDemmeltraadt's story is touchingly told amid the horrors of WWII. This work has been praised by Tom Brokaw and has also earned the New Apple Award for Excellence in Independent Publishing for 2017 as the Solo Medalist for Historical Nonfiction.

The theme of legacy writing continues with a nonfiction booklet, a clear and concise how-to manual called *Capturing Your Story: Writing a Memoir Step by Step*. Gloria lives and writes in mid-Minnesota. Contact her through her website: gloriavan.com.

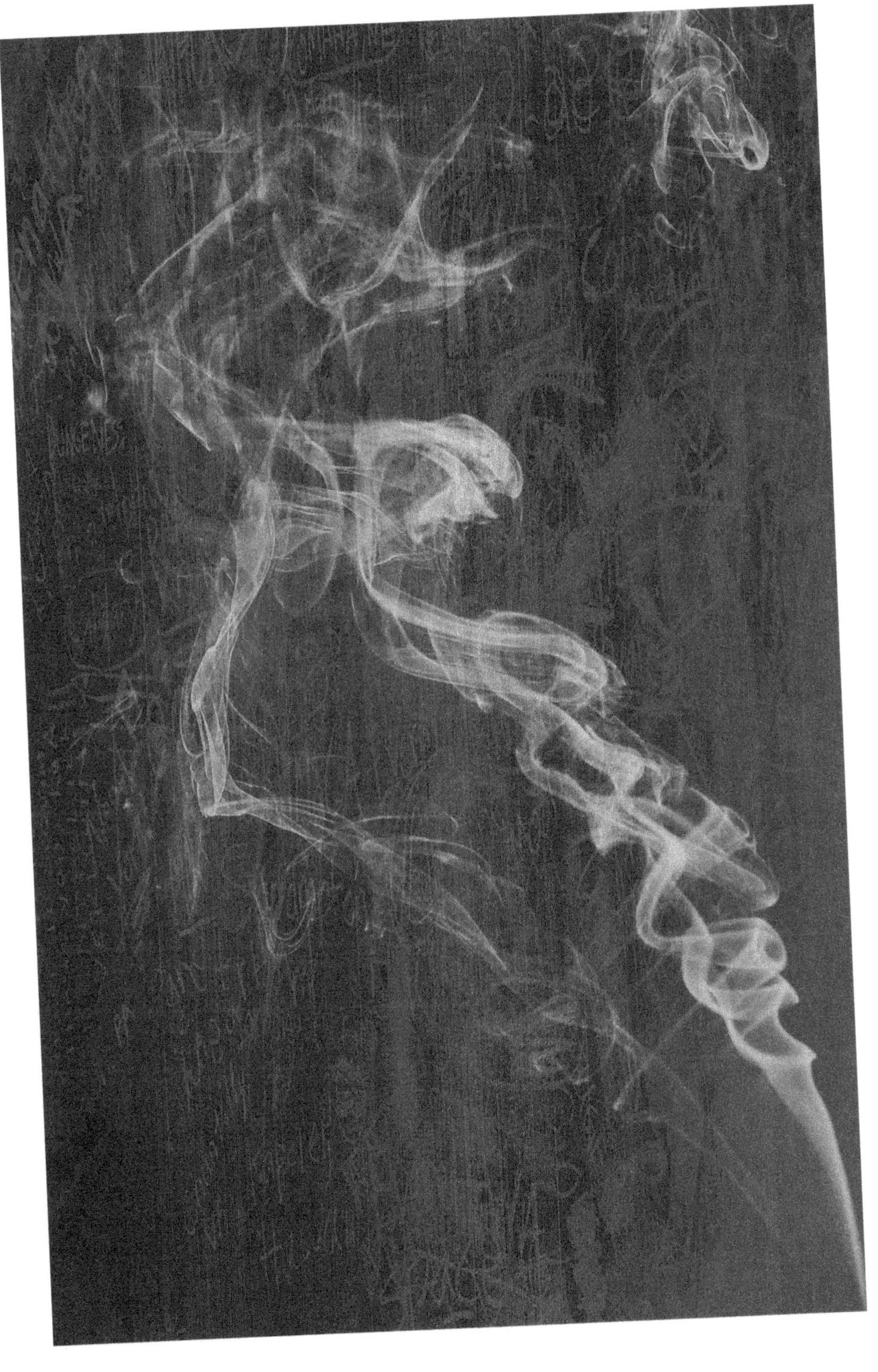

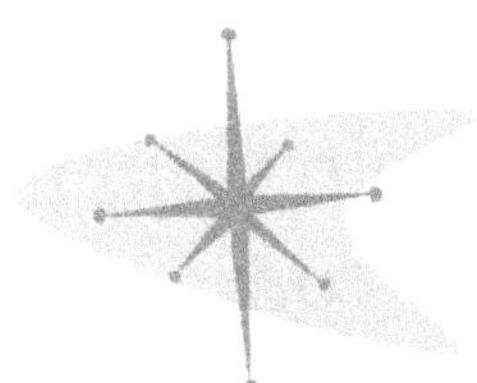

STORY EIGHT
A Presence in the House
By Lynn Garthwaite

Our real estate agent was already waiting for us in the driveway of the home she had listed for sale. When I thought about it later, I realized that the cute and clean exterior was not representative of the horrors we would find inside. This would be the 13th home we'd tour, but most notably, it was definitely the strangest. And I was never going to live there.

My husband and I had been married for four years and rented a small apartment on the north side of downtown. We liked the interesting neighborhood, and the easy walk to small, family-owned restaurants, a laundromat, and a Piggly Wiggly just around the corner. For the first year, I had lived in the apartment alone when Frank joined the army and went to Korea to serve. He came home last year, 1953, with shrapnel in his leg, but his sense of humor intact.

We greeted Diane, the realtor, and I walked in the front door of the little bungalow styled home, determined to like everything about the house so that we could stop the endless search. Frank was a good provider, working his way up the ladder at UNIVAC. With help from the G.I. Bill and my work as a typist for an insurance company, we had just enough extra money for a down payment. At the end of each work day, I came back to the apartment looking much like I did when I left in the morning. Frank came home with pieces of paper chads stuck to his clothes from the punch card room at work.

Diane led us into the small entryway in the home, and I instantly felt light headed, and found myself needing to draw in a breath. There was something really wrong here, although nothing that my eyes could see. The home was small, but neatly kept, and the furnishings were basic, but old. The layout of the entry area was odd, which added to my feelings of unease, although I couldn't figure out why.

"This area might have been used as a tv room," Diane was explaining. I looked in the direction she was pointing—a small alcove just off the main entry. It had a step down to the little area, probably only eight feet by eight feet, and I was startled to see a dark form in the corner, not with any clear edges, but it had the shape and bearing of a tall man. The dark shadowy figure moved a little, lifting his arm as if to point, and I felt an overwhelming anger coming from him. I stared, then looked away, then looked back to see if it was really there. The form stood there for a few seconds before it melted into the wall.

As my mind processed what I had seen, I realized that Frank and Diane were talking.

"A room that small and you'd almost have to be a part of the tv," Frank said, his trademark grin directed toward Diane. *He didn't see it*, I thought. *Diane didn't see it either*. I kept my mouth shut, knowing from experience that there were moments during which things that were clear as day in front of me, others denied seeing. It had been that way my entire life, as long as I could remember, but today was different. Other sightings had felt benign. I never had the sense of foreboding as I had right in that house.

Diane, oblivious to my discomfort, gaily pointed out the large window in the main living area, and then through an open doorway into the kitchen.

He's here again. I felt him, but I looked around and didn't see anyone, or any shape or form. Previously I would usually see them like a shadow, but every other time they've been surrounded by the loveliest light, and the feeling that everything about them is peace. This was different. This one made me want to run from the house, but then I looked at Frank, gazing out the window at the backyard, a telling smile on his face as he looked at a small picnic table tucked in under a giant elm tree.

He turned to look at me. I knew exactly what he was thinking. The yard would be great for kids. Those kids we had been talking about. I always said I wanted a boy and then twin girls. He would always laugh at that, as if we could plan anything that specific. He would then swoop me into the biggest hug and say "Kathy, my dear, I'd want any children that you can give me. In any order."

I was thinking about that, as I watched him smile. I wanted to warn him about the danger, but how could I say it? "Honey, there's some creepy guy that is definitely dead but is haunting this house."

I realized then that Frank was saying something, and I refocused. He was pointing to a door in the corner of the kitchen. "What's in there?" he was asking. I wanted to scream "Don't open it. Don't let it out!" knowing full well that spirits were never barricaded by anything as simple as a door. But before I could figure out what to say, Diane was opening the door and both she and Frank were peeking inside.

"Nice. A broom closet. Really handy when a box of cereal spills all over the floor." Frank looked at me, expecting a laugh, or at least a smile. I managed a weak one, still reeling from that trepidation I felt at the moment they opened that door.

Am I going crazy? Why do I feel such a heaviness in my chest? Is this what a heart attack feels like? Keep it together, Kathy.

Diane had forged on to show us the next part of the house. We walked down a short hallway in which she pointed out a small bathroom, two small bedrooms, and then a larger bedroom at the end of the hallway.

Again, what an odd layout. The stairway down to the basement began in that bedroom! And not even behind a door. The open staircase was right there as if it was a feature of the room. It took up a good portion out of what was not a particularly large room to begin with, but who designed a house in which the stairs to get to the basement were in a bedroom?

Diane was saying something about how unusual she knew this looked, but rambled something about the home builder not wanting to carve out space in the already smallish living room. Still, just looking at that stairway, knowing that it led to the basement, creeped me out.

I kept looking around, trying to spot that gray form again, as if knowing where he was made us any safer than not knowing. I suspect that both Frank and our realtor assumed I was just taking in all of the features of the house, but I was really ghost hunting.

Frank started down the steps and I think my warning came out as a kind of unintelligible groan, because both Frank and Diane turned to look at me.

"I don't think we should go down there," I managed. Diane tried to be reassuring.

"Don't worry. An inspector has come through here and he said the basement is in good shape, and there aren't any signs of any mice or ... anything."

"Mice I could handle," I said. "Did he say anything about ghosts?" I blurted it out without thinking.

Diane laughed, assuming I was joking.

"No sign of Casper, the Friendly Ghost here, although wouldn't that be fun?"

I looked at Frank, who was now studying me carefully. I hadn't told him much about the things I saw all my life. I tried to bring it up a couple of times, but I could tell he was a skeptic, like most people I knew. I had read about the Oracles of Delphi when I was in school, and when I told a friend that I thought I was an Oracle, she teased me about it relentlessly. When I talked to my mom about it, she was much kinder and, in fact, revealed that she had some of the same visions, but just never told anyone. She had cautioned me then, to just keep it to myself, because no one wants to hear that you can see ghosts, unless you're watching Casper on TV.

I made up my mind at that moment that if I was ever going to share my visions with anyone, it was going to be with Frank, the love of my life.

But not right now. Right now, all I wanted to do was get out of this house.

"Diane," I spoke up. "Thanks for showing us the house, but for several reasons, this one just isn't going to work for us."

I looked at Frank who was still standing on the stairway. I loved the look in his eyes. He may not have known what I see, but he understood how I felt. He turned and came back up the steps.

"I agree with Kathy. This one isn't for us. But we're still excited to find our forever home. Let's meet up again in a few days and keep looking."

Diane pretended that this was all fine with her. I know she was tired of showing houses to the same couple over and over again, and perhaps the 14th home would be the charm for us. But for right now, we all headed out the door and to our cars.

Four days later we got a call from Diane that she had a cute little house to show us that was only about a mile from where we lived now. Close enough to still shop at the same Piggly Wiggly!

"Oh, and by the way," she added. That house we just looked at a few days ago? I heard from my friend who works for the local paper that a woman had murdered her husband in that house. It seems that he had been abusive for years, and when he came at her one night, she shot him, right in that little alcove we saw by the front door. Strange, huh?"

Yep, strange. But I could have predicted something like that had happened. For whatever reason he just didn't want to leave that house, or, apparently, let anyone else live there either.

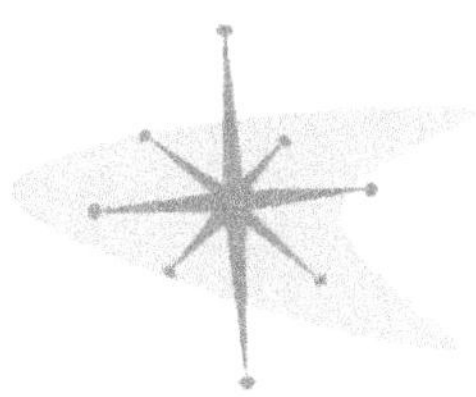

About the Author

Lynn Garthwaite is the author of eleven books, including the Dirkle Smat adventure book series, three picture books for clients (Radio Flyer and Shutterfly), and a historic nonfiction for all ages titled *Our States Have Crazy Shapes: Panhandles, Bootheels, Knobs and Points*. She has also written a mystery/thriller, *Starless Midnight,* and an updated nursery rhyme book titled *Childhood Rhymes for Modern Times*. In 2022, *Your Children Can be Writers: 40 Story Prompts to Spark their Creative Genius* was released. Lynn is also a copyeditor for three magazines, a publisher, and a member of Sisters in Crime.

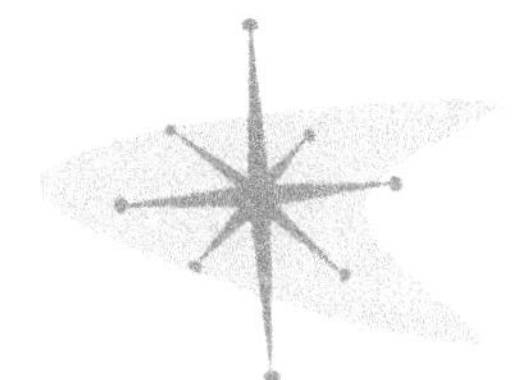

STORY NINE
Cabin 12
Susan Schussler

Fog rises eerily off the lake, spreading into every low-lying nook and culvert before submerging what it touches under a thick white blanket. The heavy mist is typical for this time of year when the lake water is warmer than the crisp fall morning air, but today's cloud brings an unease, reminding me of the water's killing past. I haven't thought much about the lake's history in the last couple of years, but on the tenth anniversary of the accident, I can't help but think about what happened to the families of the two kids who drowned in the lake. Their loss isn't that different from mine. When a loved one dies suddenly, it's always hard to accept.

A retching sob takes over my chest, pulling in the sweet aroma from my coffee with a hint of musk from the fog, and I swallow to stop the tears. I sip the hot liquid in my cup, fighting the sadness inside me. Kevin loved my parents' lake cabin. He loved watching the ducks on the lake as he sipped coffee on this old porch swing. I push back with my toes, and the long, rusted chains of the swing whine with disapproval. Kevin used to oil the swing's chains every year. I guess I need to do that now. I push back again. The chains squeal even louder, adding to the creepy feel of the morning fog.

Setting my coffee cup on the porch railing, I head into the cabin to find the oil can. There's no time like the present. I grab it with a torn wash rag from the cupboard in the back hall. The swing glides silently with a few squirts and a little wiping to catch the excess. I sit back on the swing with my coffee, feeling as if Kevin would be proud of me. I can almost feel the warmth of his body next to me, even as my mind tells me we'll never share this swing again.

"Hi." A girl's face emerges from the white mist next to the porch railing.

Startled, I jerk, sending hot liquid onto my lap. I stand quickly, forcing the coffee, with a flick of my hand, to bead down my blue cotton dress onto the floor before it could soak in and burn me.

"I'm sorry. I didn't mean to scare you," says the girl as she steps onto the porch. Her dark hair is pulled back in a ponytail, and she looks no older than twelve. She's wearing a red and white swimsuit that makes me want to wrap her in a blanket because of the morning chill. "I was just wondering if you've seen my dog." She holds up a leather leash. "He's black with white on the tip of his tail. Have you seen him?"

"Where did you come from?" I thought I was alone on the lake. The Anderson's and Olsen's cabins are closed for the season, and no one's ever at the Walden Resort. I set my coffee cup on the railing, so I don't keep spilling it.

"The Resort."

"I thought the resort was closed." Mother mentioned they were thinking about selling it.

"It must be open. We're there." She looks out into the fog. "Bingo usually comes when I call, but the fog confuses him. So you haven't seen a dog?"

"No, I haven't seen a dog. Where did you last see Bingo?"

"On the dock at the resort."

Maybe the lake *is* a killer. It killed two children. Why not a dog? "Could he have fallen into the water?"

"Naw. He's a good swimmer. He's just hiding. We're supposed to leave tonight, and I don't think he wants to go." The girl sits on the swing and pats the bench for me to join her.

Her boldness makes me smile, and as I sit next to her, a warmth that my brain recognizes as love fills my body, and because I haven't felt it in so long, I close my eyes, relishing the comfort for several seconds. When I glance at the girl, her lips are pursed, and she lets out a small giggle. "Do I know you?"

"I don't think we've met. I'm Lizzy, and you're Joanna."

Mother must have asked Mrs. Walden to keep an eye on me since I'm at the cabin alone. She mentioned talking to Mrs. Walden last week. I don't blame Mother. She worries about me even more since Kevin died. My fingers automatically find the wedding band hanging loosely on my left hand. It's been almost two years, and I still can't take it off.

"You miss him, don't you?"

I'm taken aback by her intimate knowledge of my problems, but I wouldn't put it past Mother to share my life story with anyone who will listen. She probably talked Mrs. Walden's ear off and maybe even this girl's.

"My husband, Kevin? Yes, I miss him. We'd been together since we were fourteen. We got married a week after I turned eighteen, and we were supposed to grow old together, but a year later, he was gone. I don't know how to be without him."

"He's still with you." She nods comfortingly.

"I know, in my heart. That's what my mother always says."

"If you're lonely, you should come to the resort. Everyone is very welcoming there, especially Danny."

"Danny Walden? I haven't seen him since the summer of the...."

"The accident. No one's seen much of him for the last ten years. He and his family have only been to the resort a couple of times since Danny's brother Jimmy drowned. I guess the loss was too much to stomach. But Danny's been up most of the summer working on the cabins, updating them for next spring. Ten years of neglect takes its toll on a resort." The girl stands. Holding up the dog leash, she says, "I should go. Bingo won't find himself. Come over to the resort this afternoon. Even with all the people there, I think Danny's lonely too. I'm sure he would love to see you."

"Maybe I will." I smile, standing out of politeness. As I sip my coffee, I wonder if she'll find her way back to the resort through the fog, and then I realize the sun has already started to burn it off the lake. She waves from the edge of the lawn, and I wave back. She's sweet, and I wish I were more like Lizzy — willing to put myself out there to meet new people. All my friends have avoided me since Kevin died. Either they don't know what to say or think I'll break if they say the wrong thing. The girls and I used to go out all the time. It's been months since I've met one of them for ice cream. That's probably why my ring's so loose.

After noon, I grab a sweater and the untouched plate of chocolate chip cookies my mother sent with me and head to the Walden Resort. *My life isn't going to change unless I change it.*

Following the dirt path that, over the years, has only been kept open by the deer and other animals using the trail, I find my way through the woods. The resort's tucked back in a bend in the shoreline, giving it a private bay that can't be seen from our cabin, but it's not far. When I reach the resort's clearing, my skin warms with the comfort I felt on the swing with Lizzy. I have a good feeling about coming here. I need to get out and talk to people. I've spent too much time wallowing in sadness.

The resort looks like a Norman Rockwell painting on the cover of the Post. The boats are on shore, but the dock is still out, and the grounds are full of activity. Lizzy must have found Bingo because she and a boy chase a black dog as it barks playfully. I'm glad Lizzy found him. An older couple with grey hair relaxes in white Adirondack chairs near the shore, watching the kids. They must be Lizzy's grandparents. Not far from the couple, two twenty-something women in long skirts sit at a picnic table, a chess board between them. They're arguing fiercely, but I can't hear what they're saying.

Danny Walden pounds with a hammer on a slab of wood siding, removing the nails. He looks the same as he did ten years ago when I had a schoolgirl's crush on him, but he's filled out more, matured. His thick dark hair, blue eyes, and golden tan stand out against his white t-shirt and jeans. He barely looks up as I approach with my plate of cookies.

"Hello. Lizzy told me to stop by."

"If you need a place to stay, all that I ask is you find one of the cabins that haven't been remodeled. I think numbers eight and eleven are unoccupied." He flips the board over and starts pulling the nails out with the claw end of the hammer.

"I don't need a place to stay. My parents own the grey cabin through the woods." I point to the deer trail. "I'm Joanna Burns." I give him my maiden name because he won't recognize my married one.

Danny sets the hammer down and looks up at me again. "I'm sorry, Joanna. No one told me." He combs his hand through his dark hair with a sympathetic stare, his brows furrowed. "What happened?"

I twist my wedding band nervously. He must mean what happened to Kevin. "The helicopter my husband was on crashed in Vietnam. He'll be gone two years in November. I figured your mom would have told you."

He stares at me for a minute and then directs his gaze behind me. I spin around, expecting to see a deer or a raccoon following me from the trail, but nothing's there.

"Oh." He lets out a shocked gasp. "I'm sorry." He reaches out and touches my shoulder. "When you said Lizzy sent you, I just assumed. She's always bringing strays back to the resort."

"Strays? Like her dog Bingo?"

"Never mind." He shakes his head. "Forget I said that. I could use a break. Should I fetch some milk to go with the cookies?"

"That'd be lovely."

"Don't go anywhere." He rushes toward the lodge and then turns, walking backward as his eyes meet mine. "I'll be right back. Promise you won't leave."

When I nod, he hurries up the steps into the lodge building. He looks pretty excited. The cookies are good, but not that good. They're much better warm. I hope he's not disappointed when he tries them. I set the plate on the nearest picnic table and sit in front of it on the bench. I don't want to embarrass myself struggling with the wrap in front of

Danny, so I peel it off while he's gone. When he returns with two medium size glasses of milk and sets one in front of me, he's all smiles. It's a big contrast from the bored expression he was wearing when I first arrived.

Danny wipes the sweat from his brow with the back of his hand as he sits on the bench across from me.

"So." He straightens and leans toward me with his elbows on the table. His smile's so bright it lights up his face. "You can see them."

I look down at the cookies. "They're chocolate chip."

"I mean, you talked to Lizzy, right?"

I nod. "I brought enough cookies for everyone. Should we invite them over?"

"Everyone." He chuckles. "I thought I was the only one who could see them, talk to them. I was seriously thinking about checking myself into the hospital. I thought I was going crazy. But, you can see them. We can't both be crazy."

"See who?"

"Lizzy, Mr. and Mrs. Anderson in the Adirondack chairs, the bicker sisters. That's not their real name, but they're always arguing, and I don't think I've ever gotten a last name on them. Can you see a boy with dark hair near the beach?"

What is he getting at? I look over to the beach. "The one who looks about ten?" It's the only boy I see.

"That's my little brother Jimmy. He and Lizzy drowned in 1958. I tried to save them but couldn't find them in the fog. I can't see or talk to Jimmy. Lizzy says he's here. Sometimes she tells me what he says."

I don't understand. The people at the resort are dead? I look back and forth between Danny and the people near the beach. "They're dead? Lizzy seemed so real."

"She is real. We can't share a hallucination. The bummer of it is not seeing the ones you love most. I guess that's how it works. Otherwise, you'd be able to see the guy in army fatigues on the bench next to you."

I turn to the seat next to me, but I don't see anyone. "Kevin's here?" I'm not sure why I'm whispering.

"Yeah. He says his name's Kevin. I know this is hard for you to grasp. It took me most of the summer to accept, and I'm not sure I accept it yet."

Kevin's here. I slowly lift my arm, holding it out straight to where I imagine Kevin's heart to be. I close my eyes, feeling for him. Warmth fills me, and I breathe in, relishing in it. He is here. "I have so much to tell him."

"Then tell him. He can hear you." Danny raises an eyebrow. "You just can't hear him."

"I've missed you," I whisper. "I need you. I don't know how to live without you." Tears bud in my eyes, and I bite my lip, trying to be strong, but I can't stop the tears from falling. I've waited so long to talk to him.

"Kevin says you *can* live without him. He called you sunshine."

I smile because that was his nickname for me.

"You've lived almost two years not knowing he was at your side. You can keep going. He's seen how strong you are. You deserve a good life, and he knows you'll find your way without him."

"He sounds as if he's leaving. Why does Kevin sound like he's leaving?"

"He says he was never meant to stay in this life forever. He only stayed to make sure you'd be all right, and you are now. It's time for him to go. He has other duties."

"I don't want you to go, Kevin."

"He loves you."

Tears drip from my chin, and I dab the back of my hand under my eyes. I just found him, and he's leaving again.

"Excuse me, Ma'am."

I look up to see a ten-year-old Jimmy Walden standing next to the table.

"I'd like to say goodbye to my brother. Kevin says he'll take us to where we need to go."

I understand now. Kevin needs to lead these souls to where they all belong. He's always been driven by duty. When his country called him to serve, he didn't burn his draft card. Instead, he poured all he had into the army and gave his life. I look to where Kevin is sitting and mouth, "I love you," and I swear I can feel his hand grasp mine.

Then I turn to Danny. "Jimmy wants to say goodbye. He's right here." I hold out my hand toward Jimmy since Danny can't see him.

"Please tell him I don't blame him for not rescuing me. It wasn't his fault, and he needs to stop blaming himself."

I relay Jimmy's words, and now, Danny's eyes well with tears.

He nods. "Okay." Danny's quiet for a moment before looking toward his brother. "I'll leave cabin twelve empty if you ever want to come back."

"They won't be back," I tell Danny, and Jimmy nods. I don't know how I know, but I do. I feel Kevin's hand release mine.

Then Danny and I watch as the group walks into the last patch of fog at the far end of the property and disappears. I wipe my eyes and smile at Danny, knowing neither of us will tell another person about what happened today. Who would believe us if we did?

Danny takes a cookie off the plate and dunks it into his milk. "We're never selling this place." He takes a bite of the cookie and smiles. "And I don't care what anyone says. Cabin 12 will always be empty for lost souls who need a place to stay."

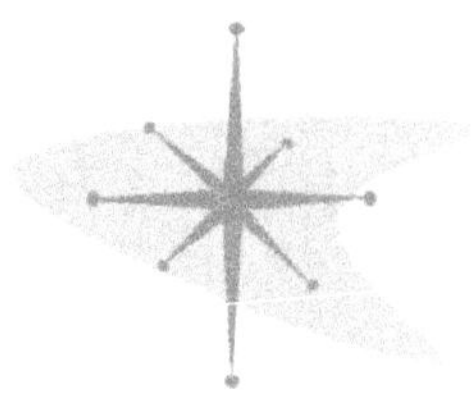

About the Author

Susan Schussler writes realistic love stories full of twists and turns. Inspired by years of working directly with others in nutrition and nursing, her characters often resemble the girl next door or someone you'd swear you know from school. Her first book, *Between the Raindrops*, debuted in 2013, and she's been writing novels ever since.

Schussler lives in Minnesota with her husband and children. And though she hates to admit it, when she's not writing or on one of Minnesota's gorgeous lakes, you may find her catching up on celebrity news. Find her online at https://susanschussler.com

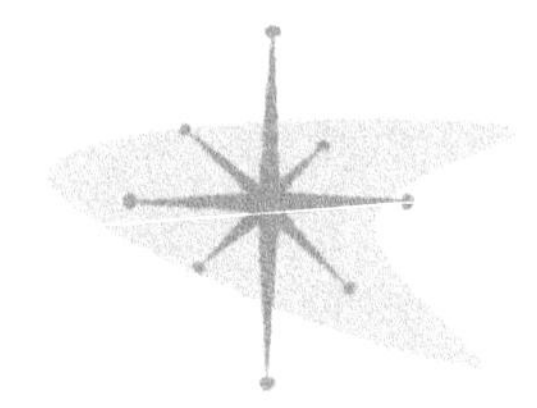

Conclusion

Thank you for reading *Reminisce Ghost Stories Book 3.* We hope you enjoyed the stories.

Watch for the next books in our Reminisce series to be released. They will be announced on our website. www.kirkhousepublishers.com